WICKED WATER

an American primitive

Other Books by MacKinlay Kantor

God and My Country
Arouse and Beware
The Romance of Rosy Ridge
Here Lies Holly Springs
Valedictory
Happy Land
The Noise of Their Wings
Glory for Me
Midnight Lace
One Wild Oat
Signal Thirty-Two
Wicked Water
Gentle Annie
Don't Touch Me
The Goss Boys
Turkey in the Straw
Lobo
Frontier
The Unseen Witness
Spirit Lake
Story Teller
Beauty Beast
Angleworms on Toast
Hamilton County
Children Sing
I love You, Irene
The Valley Forge
Gettysburg
But Look the Morn

WICKED WATER

an American primitive

MacKinlay Kantor

SPEAKING VOLUMES, LLC
NAPLES, FLORIDA
2017

Wicked Water

ISBN 978-1-62815-615-7

To Ned Brown

WICKED WATER

an American primitive

One

A huntsman was stalking buffalo through the heat and dust that covered Pearl City. He worked his way amid a jungle of loose-leaning boards and rainwater-barrels once soggy but now curling and splitting in the summer's dryness. He scrambled over stoops and past trash-boxes, his weapon ready in hand, his quarry herding ahead of him.

Through windows of the Glad Hand saloon, where dirty nine-paned frames were drawn up in their loose troughs and supported by sticks, the solid conversation of male voices drifted out to Willie Stiver's ears, and yet was unnoticed by him. He progressed stealthily a foot at a time, condensed in his imagining: he did not even wince when an old nail pierced the softer cuticle between his stony toes, and punctured his skin in a shallow wound.

Willie would die of a wound, but not one made by any nail: the germs that lurked in places like this were not stout enough to slay him. It would take a greater concentration of avarice, of cruelty and dementia, to finish off Willie Stiver.

. . . Sparrows fluttered away from him just at the

3

moment his fingers pressed the stone in his sling-shot and the rubber bands stretched and paled. Sparrows whisked carelessly around the corner, past the steps of the front platform; in a shallow tub of Pearl City's street dust they began to bathe their brown feathers.

Willie crept after them, and once again he was ready to shoot, and once again the whole covey of sparrows rose and vanished momentarily with a tiny slapping and squeaking.

They had been disturbed by the approach of a dusty horse and a rider, and thus Willie gazed upon these newcomers resentfully. He stood scowling, his knobby bare feet pressed against the heated planks, his loose underlip thrust forward. In this pose the eyes of the stranger found and scorned him.

Willie was aware, with the inarticulate intelligence of his age, that this tall rider, now coming up and dismounting at the hitch-rail, would see before him only a dirty fourteen-year-old youth, with a stained red-and-white-striped sweater, with skinny bare legs angling down from the unbuttoned slits of his filthy knickerbockers. He would not see the woodsman and trapper, hot on the trail of grizzlies that lurked amid these canyons.

Idly the stranger whipped a halter-knot around a rail from which the bark had been peeled by a thousand such tetherings and more. This young man was big of bone, sullen and dark of face; yet his eyes—however antagonistic—carried deep inside them a constant and futile asking for mercy. His horse had an expensive

4

saddle, though one well-worn; a valise and a slicker were tied behind it.

The man himself was even more shabby than the furniture of his horse. He wore the coat of a cheap brown business suit, with dark blotches of perspiration under the arms. His tight denim trousers (to be called levis in other years and places) hung faded outside his high-heeled boots.

"Scared them away!" muttered Willie Stiver, in hatred of this rider who had frightened his prey.

The man dusted himself with an old flat-crowned hat. "What did you say, kid?"

"Didn't say nothing."

His eyes had frightened Willie; yet dimly in this agitation, Willie felt that he was as much dismayed by the hopeless pleading in the young man's glance as by the actual implied menace.

The stranger walked into the Glad Hand saloon. Willie, watching through the open doorway where slatted doors were held wide by a couple of tilted chairs, could observe the man in the denim pants waiting motionless until his eyes had become accustomed to the comparative gloom. Finally he moved out of the boy's sight, on toward the bar; and Willie, resuming his hunt and holding his sling-shot ready, advanced into the heat waves of the rutted street.

Within the Glad Hand, eyes other than Willie's now watched the newcomer as he stepped forward for refreshment. Three of the more prosperous cattlemen of the region were seated at a rear table with the railroad station agent. A variety of lading bills, stock receipts

5

and other papers were spread among their beer glasses.

The men were Jaff Montgomery, sallow and black-browed; John Britton, prim and rather terse-spoken as to manner; and Peter Alesworth, whose bald head and moon-face gave an impression of geniality. All of them wore the heavy watch-chains, the diamond-studded charms, the glaring signet rings and other trappings of their kind. The stamp of an angrily-won success was on them all.

The Glad Hand was decorated on its interior with heads, muzzles, the rigid wings of a hoard of beasts and birds, but the dust of twenty-two years was thick upon most of these. False eyes gazed down, the dry lips and tongues were degenerated into an unwholesome duskiness, and tiny insects had been at work upon many of the specimens, to pit their fur and jag their wings.

At the rear a stiff staircase, its rail polished by multitudes of sweaty hands, rose to a platform and a closed door at the top. The light and nervous feet of performers, the tapping heels of hostesses—and in the old days the heavy boots of men who stamped upward in their lust—these had worn the steps into lumps. The structure hung there identical with the past, hopeless against the present and the future.

Before a jumbled forest of bottles Ole Paulson waited for the stranger's order. Ole was the fifth proprietor in line of succession at the Glad Hand, yet even he had lived long in Pearl City. No matter how many strangers came through that door, he could now be a partner to the subconscious resentment which men in remote and thinly-peopled towns bore against each face projected

6

to them in its newness, against each voice that spoke in sharply unfamiliar tones . . . there was always the wonder, the suspicion sometimes mingled with fear and always with a rejection: a ruling-out, until the newcomer might be admitted to familiarity solely through protraction of his presence.

The air of the saloon waited hot. The few men standing at the bar turned back slowly to contemplate their drinks or to glance covertly at one another.

Peter Alesworth began to speak at the littered table, but even he lowered his voice because a stranger now stood near. He said to the agent, "Then, on the 17th, I'll need five more cars—maybe six. I'm shipping at least that many head."

John Britton touched the close-clipped brush of his gray mustache. "I'll need ten cars on the 20th, myself." His eyes were still on the black-haired man at the bar.

Jaff Montgomery pronounced in a whisper the query of their common mind. "Who's that fellow just came in?"

They could all look with freedom now.

"Never saw him before."

The stranger, his eyes focused through the gloom, was regarding them stare for stare, and with an air of contemptuous boldness which none of them would ever be able to command if he lived to be a hundred . . . none of them would live that long.

He had halted, resting an elbow on the shiny wood of the bar, and his attitude thus pushed the shabby brown coat-skirts aside. Jewels of revolver cartridges shone in a gold studding on his belt, and voiced the unspoken challenge of such armament to any man choosing to controvert him.

Ole Paulson moved up behind the bar. "Something for you?"

"Shoot me with two cannonballs."

"What?"

"Couple of cannonballs."

"Oh," said Paulson, comprehending. He found a bottle of Jas. Cannon's Sour Mash in front of the bar mirror, and placed two liquor glasses before the dark-faced man. Cautiously he filled both glasses to the brim; only one drop was spilled; it lay like a ruddy pearl.

Some customers who entered the Glad Hand were empty of pocket: there had been trouble of that kind before. . . .

"That'll be fifty cents, mister."

"Twenty-five cents a drink? That's too high."

The querulous, falsely-laughing corners of Paulson's mouth turned up and down again. "Freight rates are high, too, mister." He inclined his head cutely toward the station agent as he said it.

The big young stranger brought out an old-fashioned purse with a reticule snap. He untwisted the snap, delved into the interior, and produced a half-dollar which thudded and rang upon the bar. Paulson accepted the money and moved away, but he took the whiskey bottle with him.

Again the stranger turned, aware of the continued stares of the few loafers and the men at the table. He regarded them with calm as he drank one glass of the whiskey at a gulp. He drank every drop: there was

8

scarcely enough moisture left to ring the bar as he turned the little glass upside down in front of him. Casually he lifted the second glass, addressing Paulson as he did so.

"My horse is pretty played out. Got a good livery stable around here?"

Ole Paulson nodded and managed to shrug at the same time. "Stiver's livery stable. It's right around in back of the saloon here. I wouldn't say it's too good, but it'll probably do."

Silence lay hard between them.

"What you mean is—it'll do for people like me?" asked the stranger.

The Scandinavian proprietor, slight of frame and in no way combative as to nature, preferred to disregard any challenge implied. He indicated the front door. "I saw Stiver's kid out in front a while ago. Guess he could show you where it is."

The customer drank half of his second whiskey, and then turned toward the front door. When he came out, he found Willie Stiver still trying to kill a sparrow. Birds had returned to squabble over the fresh droppings behind the stranger's own horse; Willie had fired once and missed. Now he had found what he thought was better ammunition: a stubby bolt dropped from some wagon. With this bullet squeezed in the leather patch of his sling-shot, he was concentrating on his aim.

"Hey, kid," the stranger called, and the sparrows rose and fled.

"That's my horse, there at the rail. Take him around to your Pa's livery barn and tell him to water him easy, and give him a good rub."

9

Willie cried, in the distilled fury of this second resentment, "Aw, who was your slave last year?"

He scooted under the railing and down into the street, where he made as hideous a face as his natural lineaments would permit—and that was hideous enough; he was an ugly boy to begin with.

After a moment, the stranger finished his drink and went back into the saloon. He knew that the men inside had heard every word spoken, and thus he felt embarrassment as he returned to the bar. No matter how cheap and worn-out his clothing, he held the attitude of a man unaccustomed to having his orders flouted by anyone—more especially by a small boy.

His laugh tittered out dryly, without humor.

"You got some pretty smart-alecky kids in Pearl City. Give me another drink—another couple." His big brown hand held the purse ready to pay.

Out in the street the sparrows had not returned; they found other attractive provender scattered far down the road in front of the Continental House, and there they bickered and fed.

Willie gazed at the tiny, distant birds, scampering like thick-bodied moths, and he considered a foray into that down-the-street neighborhood. But recollection of the fact that he was even here straying from the premises where he had been ordered to remain, held him to the vicinity of the Glad Hand.

He had been set to ladling oats with a peck measure, filling up a tin bushel-basket, lugging the basket to the new oat bin (which Garrett Stiver, his father, hoped he had made rat-proof), dumping the contents therein,

10

going back for more oats. . . . It was a hot and tiring job, also a prickly one, for the pointed granules had a way of sifting through Willie's cotton sweater, tickling and stabbing around his waist as the boy worked. There was nothing in this world hotter and drier than old oats —unless it was the blown, baked earth of the town and the drying plains beyond. Gare Stiver had been summoned to the wagon-works at the other end of town, and doubtless had not yet returned to his livery barn; even so, it might be some time before he thought to check up on his son and the business of the oat bin.

There was yet time to play and pursue, to fire out the missiles in flat trajectory from his sling-shot, to see glass smash if he struck his target . . . and in fancy see a mountain lion drop inert at Willie's very feet, and to hear the gruff voice of an imagined guide exclaiming, "Ugh, good shot."

Flat before the platform of the Glad Hand lay an empty bottle; thick-grained, short-necked, with a gold label plastered against its emptiness. Willie picked up the bottle; the label read: *B. Linn's Blackberry Cordial*, and Willie sniffed and found the scent tantalizing.

This one target he would destroy, and then scoot back to his tiresome task in the livery barn.

Cautiously the boy placed the bottle upright, not on the hitch-rail—it was round, and trembling at times to the stamp of the stranger's horse; but on the flat wooden streamer which made a fence between posts of the saloon canopy.

Willie backed into the street, and saw the bottle waver and disappear before his eyes. A Cheyenne Indian loomed there, decked with war paint, adorned with the blood of several fresh scalps . . . this was such an Indian as had slain Willie's grandfather, no doubt—perhaps the identical brave. Menacing face pushed closer, bronze lips twisted in a snarl, the tomahawk was raised on high . . . Willie cocked his Winchester and took steady aim. He fired; the Indian tottered, collapsed, his despairing death cry rattled among mountains. . . .

The stubby wagon bolt cracked against thick glass and spun away through the open door of the Glad Hand saloon, halting in its whizzing ricochet when it glanced smartly against the kneecap of the stranger who stood there, with Ole Paulson pouring more whiskey in front of him.

The man gave one involuntary gasp of pain; Ole and the others looked their surprise. There had been a clink of metal and glass outside, the sharp thud of the same missile striking tight cloth and skin and hard bone, the clatter against the bar, the tiny rolling on the floor. . . .

Steadily the stranger moved toward the door and out across the saloon's platform. Men watched through dimness into the outside glare. It was as if the big-shouldered young man who had glowered close at hand was now transfigured: an actor before their staring eyes—his every growl and motion played dangerously, and all this scene lighted by foot-lamps of the afternoon sun.

Willie had come up to the platform's edge, and happily he was contemplating the ruin he had made . . . should he take the Cheyenne's scalp? He had no knife. . . .

The stranger reached down past the railing, grabbed Willie so hard and hurtfully that his cheap old sweater tore, and hauled the boy up on the platform.

No one stood there to declare that the sling-shot had not been aimed directly to harry him: a mean little catapult in the hands of a child who had already flouted his edict. The stranger lifted his open hand and struck, and the banging sound of the slap tore loose a screech from Willie. The stranger struck again, slapping twice more in the expending of his fury. His face was vicious.

Slowly the white faded from tanned knuckles as his grasp relaxed; the man shoved Willie from him. The boy was fairly spouting tears.

"You big bully!" he wailed. "You didn't have to hit me . . . you didn't have to hit me!"

He stumbled away to the edge of the platform, turned for one backward look (still this might be a dream, an ugliness too overwhelming to be realized in fact). But there he was: the hard-shaven stranger, his black felt hat drawn low against his face, and the supplication still morbid in his long-lashed eyes—a spectacle more terrible than if those eyes had narrowed in hate.

Willie Stiver fled away, stumbling, yelling still, his plaint intensified in the rear areaway between wooden buildings. He sought shelter at the livery stable from which feloniously he had strayed, and the stranger walked back into the saloon where his whiskey was waiting, poured again in two glasses at the bar.

Every person in the saloon had seen exactly what happened upon the platform. Some of them may have guessed, in error along with the stranger, at the childish though vexatious assault supposedly practised by Willie. Most of the men were fathers; they had been called upon to discipline their own children or others with force of superior strength. Beatings among boys and men alike were far commoner in 1899 than they came to be in a later age, when the massed barbarity of nations supplanted the insignificant sadism of the individual.

However there was something so ferocious in this young man's slow step and in the spiteful blows he hurled with his palm: a kind of studied villainy suggesting that this act was truly delightful to the instigator, and not solely prompted by a hasty reaction which would bring repentance in its train. . . .

Sheriff Ab Ballantine in particular gazed upon this hooligan with repugnance. Ballantine was a good-natured old incompetent with a love of politics, a joy of haranguing and talking in large terms (he had even been an unsuccessful candidate for the Legislature) but he had little notion of the responsibilities of his office beyond those expressed at election time in vaguely flamboyant terms.

The horny business of handling prisoners and making arrests, he delegated to his deputies in whole; it was rare for him even to speak sharply to a quarrelsome drunk, no matter what audience waited to observe. Ballantine was a physical if not a moral coward.

However, the nasty act on the sunlit stage had jarred the sheriff into a remonstrance wholly reflexive. The old man's hand shook as he squeezed beer out of his mustache and gazed the length of the bar.

14

He growled, "Why don't you pick on somebody your own size?"

Leisurely the customer tossed down his whiskey; turning his face against the brown shoulder of his coat, he hunched his shoulder and wiped his wet mouth on the cloth.

"If you were my size and my age," he told Ballantine, "I'd pick on you."

Ole Paulson filled one stoneware stein with beer, shoved it aside and thrust another stein under the spigot. Only slightly more bold than Sheriff Ballantine, he drew a strength from the attitude evinced by Ballantine.

"All right, mister. All right!" In his annoyance Paulson fell into the Swedish accent and intonation which he avoided assiduously at other times. "You had better finish up your drink and go now."

The stranger did not reply. He took up his second glass of whiskey, found a soaked bit of paper in the liquor, and impassively swished it out with his finger.

Paulson, in response to a motion from one of the men farther down the bar, went back to the spigot and lifted a fresh stein. He watched the unresponding stranger narrowly.

No matter what the strength of this solid hostility facing him, the young man turned to stare at the others with a bullying assurance that made them seem not evenly matched, but actually weaker in power than he.

The stranger's name was Buster Crow. At birth he had been called Buswell, after his mother's people in the semi-wilderness of a distant state, and logically his nickname was Bus. Now he seldom used the patronymic which had become his Christian name. Bus Crow had never been in Pearl City before; but he was held in fear, sometimes in interest, and by many people in loathing, in other regions nearby.

Crow glanced from face to face. Coolly his contemptuous eyes ranged past the people and assayed the wooden panels where hung mounted heads and fleeces of a menagerie: coyote fangs, bear teeth, antlers, dried parchment of snakeskins, horns of wild sheep . . . his gaze traveled mockingly over the sinister assemblage. A cougar leered at him, and a bobcat close to it. He leered back with livelier ferocity, though he did not draw up his lip and actually display the venom of his snarl.

Had anyone been standing closer to him than these disapproving patrons, it would have been possible to observe a wretchedness—a gloomy melancholy—settling over his face, but replaced rapidly by annoyance. It was as if he scented an odor he found unpleasing . . . perhaps he heard a sound. . . .

Surely a sound bubbled through the hot silence of the room; Bus Crow's eyes sought out the cause. Ole Paulson had gone down the bar carrying the last stein of beer drawn, and with his soaked wooden paddle he was wiping off surplus foam; but he had left the beer tap partially open. The liquid trickled down in a foamy icicle, spilling against the darkened zinc of the trough below.

Crow gazed as if hypnotized at the talkative beer-tap.

16

When finally he was able to speak, he stammered slightly over the first word.

"Ssshut off that faucet!"

Paulson placed beer before Sheriff Ballantine, and turned to look at Crow with stupidity. "What?"

"I said—turn off that faucet!"

There was a stir, a shuffling, the jingle of loose spurs when some of the men moved their feet—then the slow plod-plod of Paulson's footsteps as he came back to the bar tap, clamped the faucet shut, and observed that the foamy yellow stream ceased to flow.

He shook his head at the stranger in complete mystification. "What ails you, anyway? What's eating you?"

Crow swallowed before he could reply. A constriction of quivering muscles showed beneath the skin of his cheeks, jaw and neck.

"I simply don't like to hear a little trickle of water running, that's all."

"But that ain't water, that's beer," said Paulson.

Sheriff Ballantine laughed audibly at this jest, but no one else made a sound.

From outside came a growing hubbubb: the rapid stamping of boots, the patter of bare feet mingling with them, and the loose *nyah-nyah-nyah* of a child's whimper coming toward the door.

The round-shouldered figure of Gare Stiver, the livery barn proprietor, appeared in the doorway. Gare stood blinking; he was carrying a broken-handled buggy whip.

Stiver was half-bald at thirty-eight, obviously toil-worn, unsuccessful, marked with the dirt of stables. His

17

shirt was more disgustingly stained than the clothing of his son; suspenders drawn tight over the garment were edged with black grease—decorated with little stamps of red dust where the metal adjustments had been moved and snapped shut, moved, snapped shut again at new positions as the suspenders lost their elasticity.

The boy mourned close beside the father, sobbing louder as he sensed an audience.

"He just hit me, that's all," he wailed. "I wasn't doing anything. Not anything, Pa!"

In the front of the bar, Bus Crow turned to examine the pair before him. Smoothly he settled his back against the round of the bar and held on, both hands sliding wide, gripping the mahogany.

Gare Stiver's voice broke in, harsh and nasal above the boy's sobs. "Which fellow was it, Willie?"

Willie pointed his black-nailed finger.

"Him, Pa. It was him! I wasn't doing anything—"

Gare Stiver approached Buster Crow. He would have stood taller than Crow if his shoulders had not been so bent; but he was nothing like so bulky: there was no air of impregnability about him. Face to face with the stranger, he stood breathing heavily, staring into those gray-black eyes, visibly summoning his courage.

When he spoke, it was in an explosive gasp. "What do you mean, hitting my kid? I got a good notion to—"

Nonchalantly, Bus Crow drew up his right leg, lifting the dusty boot high. With a piston-like stab he shoved the sole of his boot fairly against Gare Stiver's middle.

The whip flew away. Staggering off balance, Stiver

18

went backward for ten feet, waving his arms in an effort to arrest himself. The momentum was too great. He landed amid a pile of chairs and an upset table; a splintering crash echoed through the room.

One other table was very nearly upset: Alesworth and the other stockmen, together with the station agent, had leaped to their feet, but no one moved a step nearer the scene.

Gare rolled over on his side and held a hand tightly against himself where the kick had hurt him. He climbed into a kneeling position.

His words sounded thinner, frailer, but they were distinctly audible. "All right," he told the stranger. "if that's the way you want it! I see you're wearing a gun; wait till I go get mine."

He sucked in air and rose clumsily to his feet.

There came a cynical giggle from Bus Crow. "Listen, Baldy. Don't try any gun-play with me."

Swiftly his right hand went down to flick the tail of his old brown coat; he wrenched his revolver out of its holster.

He called to the assemblage, "Look at Bright-eyes up there."

Beyond the disordered table and chairs, high between windows, a deer stared blankly into space. Bus Crow took steady aim. He fired once, the gun kicked up, he steadied it hastily and fired again. They could see him do this; in a way it seemed to take some time, yet the two explosions were very nearly simultaneous . . . a jargon of echoes slammed back and forth.

Both of the deer's glass eyes were shattered and

destroyed; the board to which the head was nailed had a split in it. Dust sifted down, mingling with the heavy smoke of black-powder cartridges.

"You go back to your livery stable," said the stranger to Gare Stiver, "and take my horse with you. It's the chestnut with a valise tied to the saddle. Take care of him, like I bid your son a while ago."

Again that awful chuckle stole from somewhere in his corded throat. "Don't worry: I got the money to pay you. I guess you need the business."

Gare Stiver went out, herding the frightened boy ahead of him. In silence the group at the ranchers' table could observe Stiver halting on the platform for a moment; then, bent down by circumstance as he was, and humanly impressed by Crow's marksmanship, he walked obediently to the rail. He slipped under, unfastened the halter-hitch and moved out of sight, leading the stranger's horse.

Ole Paulson was the first to speak; he did so cautiously but stubbornly.

"You got to pay me for that deer."

"How much?"

"Well, it's spoiled. The board and— I don't know just what those eyes would cost."

"Then why worry about it?" asked Crow.

With reluctance the cattlemen reseated themselves. Somehow there was an anticlimax about this brawl so suddenly terminated. For a moment or two it had seemed to promise more serious repercussions than extemporaneous target-shooting.

Sheriff Ballantine picked up his beer and drank hastily. He would say nothing; but of the ranchers Jaff Montgomery was always the one most ready to speak.

He was as rich as anyone else in the region. He felt a pride in his position and recognized his responsibility toward the community at large.

Though his face was visibly more sallow than it had appeared a few minutes earlier, Jaff called across to the stranger, "Just the same, mister, I'd advise you to look out for Gare Stiver—I don't care what kind of a target-shooter you are."

Crow spun his empty whiskey glass on the counter and wiped his lips. He took a step or two toward the table, eyes glowing, though the rest of his face was as expressionless as a cow-pie.

"Folks say," Montgomery cautioned, "that Stiver has killed three men. I know for a fact he's killed one. Happened right over there at the livery barn."

Bus Crow tilted his head and let loose a bray of laughter. He wagged a finger at Ole Paulson, pale behind the closed-up spigot. "Boss, give me another drink! Just one, this time."

Crow turned back to Montgomery, and the sight of the cattlemen seemed to rekindle his amusement. He began laughing again.

They all looked at one another, then at Crow.

"Well," Montgomery challenged him, "how many people have you killed?"

The young man stopped laughing. His face turned into black stone. "Sixty-seven."

There was not even a nervous titter from anyone in

the saloon as the stranger uttered this appalling boast. Peter Alesworth drew a purple silk handerkerchief from his breast pocket and ran the crushed fabric across his forehead. "Sixty-seven," Alesworth repeated lightly. "That's quite a bunch of folks. What's your name, anyway?"

The stranger turned back toward the bar and motioned to Ole Paulson, still rooted there. "Come on with that drink." And then, over his shoulder to the ranchmen: "My name's Buster Crow."

Little voices talked all along the bar . . . voices spoke across dreary elipses of the empty tables merging throughout the open room. No one spoke a word in fact; yet the voices were there, gossiping and exclaiming from place to place, from man to man—telling their tale, not so much in terror as in delight at possessing even this unruly kinship with the notorious.

. . . Yes, yes, I've heard of him . . . who hasn't? Ha . . . used to work for that detective agency and . . . remember how Henry Kortz told about meeting Bus Crow over in Colorado, the time after he killed those . . . used to be a scout against the Indians, down in Arizona; they say he staged a private massacre . . . I read he went to fight in Cuba. . . .

The hush and whisper of the speaking tongues was busy (still no one could speak aloud).

Sheriff Ballantine swallowed down the half-a-stein of beer remaining; with stiff fingers he brushed the spilled foam from his breast.

Bus Crow leaned against the bar. "Guess you might

22

as well make it another couple of cannonballs," he said, "instead of just one."

Ole Paulson poured the drinks, but this time there was a certain amount of whiskey wasted.

Crow lifted the wet glass, held it against his lips, then lowered it.

"Happen to know where a man could get a good job?"

This was beef country. "You mean working with cattle, Mr. Crow?" asked Paulson, with a rare and trembling squeak of politeness.

"Could be."

Paulson leaned across the bar and spoke in a self-consciously intimate whisper: "Well, the big outfits—you know how it is—they're cutting down—not taking on any new men. Yes, Mr. Crow, the situation's bad. They're even letting a lot of their old hands go."

His secret little nod indicated the three cattle-raisers at the table: all staring now, with the railroad agent gaping beside them.

"Take them fellows over there. Not a one of them is running as many cattle as he did a year ago. Some of them have even been selling cows, Mr. Crow."

Bus Crow finished off the little glass and rang it down. "Selling cows? I don't get the idea."

Paulson tittered almost affectionately. "I know how it would be with you: you've been in the war—far away in Cuba and places—you don't know what's happening out here in the cattle country. But you ought to look in the paper one time, or listen to how folks talk. It's nesters—little outfits coming in—movers that have got on the land and took it up for homesteads. I tell you, Mr. Crow, they're putting up fences nowadays; and folks say that some of those people— They rustle off calves from the big outfits and put their own brands on them."

He whispered ominously, shoving himself even farther forward across the wet top of the bar to make sure that Bus Crow heard him. *"It's true."*

Crow was totally scornful of this little Swede who had been antagonistic to him only a short time previously but who now was fawning before him. Still he recognized what must be the truth of Paulson's statements.

"Doesn't sound like the job prospects were very good."

"We still got some big herds in the vicinity, Mr. Crow," said Ole Paulson. "Yes, indeed! We still got some mighty big herds."

Two

It was up on the lowest ridge wandering down from the Dog-tooth Hills, that Bob Crashaw and three of his men saw the birds gathered.

The air of early morning was thin and cool; the men did not sweat as they drove their horses forward and followed Crashaw around the rocks, quartering across the face of the easiest slope. They even turned with appreciative interest to observe the two antelopes they had startled by their clattering approach, and watch the pinkish bodies leaping across bunchy grass with such ease. Curves of their horny prongs caught a varnish from the sun. . . .

Crashaw alone did not turn to watch the antelopes capering. He was one of Jaff Montgomery's foremen: a bony man of thirty with a heavily pock-marked face. His gaudy black-and-white checked shirt, soiled by days of service, was colored to tan over the left breast pocket where cigarette tobacco had sifted from the little bags that Crashaw carried there. He was a conscientious if sullen young man, keenly aware that he would earn his foreman's wage just so long as his attention to detail won the approval of his employer.

Within six or eight minutes after they had first spotted the birds, Crashaw and his men were sitting their horses in silence, without motion, gathered at the lip of a saucer on the hillside. They gazed reflectively at the blood and horns and raw skin already alive with flies above its blood . . . ugly eye-sockets where the earliest birds had taken their juicy pickings. . . .

"Worst job of butchering I've seen yet," said Snap Hilkenberger.

Crashaw's left stirrup crunched as he stepped to the ground. "This makes the third in two days. Boss'll have a hemorrhage when we tell him."

Hilkenberger dismounted also, and scouted about for tracks. "Hoof marks here, all right."

"When I was a kid in the Dakota country," said Crashaw, "the Sioux Indians ran off some of my father's stock. Wasteful bunch of sons-of-bitches: when we found the cattle, only the tenderloins were gone. Just cut out the tenderloins: that was all the Indians wanted to carry off. You boys make a circle. Maybe we can tell which way he went. He or they."

While the others were riding about, Bob Crashaw poked close to the buzzing, smelly remains of the steer, trying to find some clue, but he was unsuccessful. The stony soil gave little help, and no implements or receptacle had been left behind by the butcher.

The men came back to report, talking without much interest. This was an old story, aggravating to their sense of pride, perhaps; but there was not one of them who, if married and homesteaded on the nearby range, would have hesitated about slaughtering an animal belonging to any of the big outfits.

Hilkenberger believed that the tracks went south toward the end of the ridge; the others were not so certain.

"South? Down below." Crashaw meditated while his tongue licked his cigarette paper. "There's that new fellow just built his house next to the old dry spring, and drilled down a well. What's his name—Miller? Guess he's got about nine head of cattle of his own. Let's get down there and take a look."

Soon they were sitting, still mounted but accusingly halted in front of a wire homestead fence, where a cubical pine house glared yellow in the heightening sun. Everything about the place smacked of newness, crudeness, cheapness. Miller had recently bought a pump, and he was endeavoring to screw the implement into place on the shaft ready for it. The cowboys could hear him tinkering from afar.

Now he faced them from inside the gate, bare-headed and scrawny, running a dirty hand through his limp hair. Up on the stoop of the house his wife gazed out belligerently.

"That's pretty serious," said Miller, "accusing me of stealing cattle—"

Crashaw said, "Nobody's accusing you of anything. We just said the trail led here."

"Why not?" retorted Miller. "I rode past there this morning early. I was in town all night, and I saw some birds around when I came past, and I wondered what

27

had happened. That doesn't prove I butchered that beef, does it?"

Crashaw spoke again. His voice was characteristically thin and flat, held on a mechanical even tone, with no rise or fall of emphasis at the termination of any sentence. "You got blood and grease on your overalls right now."

Miller glanced down at his clothing guiltily, and then lifted his head, determined to brazen the thing out. "Sure I have. Just had to shoot a cow of my own. She fell on the rocks and broke her leg. Haven't I got a right to butcher my own beef? What kind of a country is this?"

Snap Hilkenberger said, "You better be sure it's your own beef."

"Well, I am sure."

"Come on, let's get along," said Crashaw. "He's a liar, but we can't prove it." They turned their horses and rode off.

Miller advanced to the fence as they moved away, and calmly folded his arms on the top strand of tight wire as he watched his accusers—men and horses distorted by thickening heat-waves before they had traveled more than a hundred rods. . . . Miller's stringy-haired wife grinned in relief. She advanced from the house and came to stand behind her husband, folding her hands in her dirty apron. Miller grinned also.

Three

That night Jaff Montgomery, together
with John Britton and Peter Alesworth,
dined at the Stockmen's Club in Pearl
City with three other cattle-raisers of the region.
Among them it is likely that the six men represented
two-thirds of the accumulated wealth of Pearl County
—at least that portion of the accumulated wealth which
fed, bawling and branded, over the ranges, along the
streams, and herded through summer into cooler hills
as grass dried up on the plains.

Driscoll, Springstun and Webb were older men—
perhaps not so outspokenly active in state and local politics, but at least people of dignity and importance.
They, too, wore the jeweled lodge charms of their
breed, and held a traditional fondness for apple pie,
brandy and white coffee.

With these toys they were now playing. Colored
waiters worked briskly to clear away other remains of
their dinner in a little private dining chamber next to
the billiard room. The conversation had been earnestly
unhappy, and John Britton motioned for the waiter to
take away his untasted wedge of pie.

He said, "I've got half a notion to sell out."

Jaff Montgomery told him grimly, "I'm only fifty-one years old." He looked older than that. "Fifty-one's too young to quit. I don't want to sell out. I want to fight these nesters, these movers. Fight the whole bunch."

Alesworth squeezed a wet cigar to death in the marble ash-tray before him. "That would be fine, if you only knew how to do it."

"It's past the time for talk," said Montgomery. "We've been talking all during supper, and just where did it get us? Nowhere. If they keep this up—settle on our ranges, change our brands, butcher our stock—we're going to have our backs to the wall."

Old Bill Springstun muttered assent. The others sat silent and reflective, watching Montgomery. He seemed to draw vigor from their attention.

"When I say fight—I mean just that."

No one of them was under the age of forty-five—some were nearly twenty years older. They had known many degrees of violence when they were younger; but they knew too that 1899 was no longer a frontier hour; their frontier hours had already been lived. They were businessmen, and Pearl County was their place of business: the vast grassy shop where they prepared their wares and shipped them away for sale.

"The first time one of us shoots a nester," said Alesworth quietly, "that's murder."

John Britton felt the ridge of his mustache with a hard fingernail. His crisp voice split sharply the silence which followed the word "murder."

"Gentlemen, I want to go on record right now—I'm a church man, a family man. I agreed to meet tonight with you, eat supper here at the club, talk things over, see what we could do about this situation. But when you start talking *murder*—well, you can deal me out. I'd rather sell every head—go out of business entirely —than be mixed up in anything like that."

He said this simply but forcefully. The men glanced with shyness at one another, and Montgomery looked a little taken aback.

A waiter came in and approached Peter Alesworth, his cinnamon-brown face politely attentive. "Letter for you, Mr. Alesworth—just noticed it in your box. I thought you might want to have it, sir."

Alesworth didn't even look up. He sat holding the letter, listening until the waiter had gone out of the room and the door had been shut again. This was a plain white envelope with no address: merely Alesworth's name typed on the front.

He appeared fairly reluctant to tear open the envelope, though at last his fingers did obey the bidding of curiosity.

The others fell back into conversation, while Alesworth bent close above the paper, reading and re-reading. There was some talk about poker, but it was only a half-hearted interest . . . yes, it was late. Clarence Webb said that his wife was having trouble with her neuralgia again; he ought to get along home and see how she was. . . .

Alesworth folded the letter carefully, unfolded it, looked at it again. He arose, discharging without actual request a plea for silence.

"One moment, gentlemen. This is an anonymous letter. You can take turns reading it."

He passed the single typed sheet to Britton on his right.

"I don't know who wrote it," Alesworth said. "Some one of you—some one of us. It's just picked out on a typewriter. No signature."

Jaff Montgomery was the first to break the silence, while Britton still read. "Well, what does it say?"

Alesworth groped through several pockets before he could find his handkerchief—a red one, this time. He wiped his forehead and temples.

"The writer of the letter suggests that we engage Buster Crow to do the job for us—rather, the writer says that *he* will engage Bus Crow. We're each to put up two thousand dollars."

... Britton had finished reading; he shoved the letter on to Montgomery. He stared up at Peter Alesworth; his voice rose far above its natural pitch when he spoke. "Just like you said: this means murder!"

Alesworth seemed fighting a panic which sought to claim him. "Not necessarily, John. Every nester will have warning. They can either get off our ranges—stop stealing our stock and branding our calves—or they can take their medicine."

He put the damp handkerchief away and gazed at his friends as if appealing for an explanation he could not offer.

"Each of us," he said to the group, "will procure two thousand dollars in cash, and all meet here tomorrow night. The money will be placed in a single envelope,

32

and will be hidden in the billiard room, by me, at a place to be designated by the writer of this letter. He says he'll leave another note tomorrow morning or some time beforehand, telling me where to hide the envelope. Sounds like a kind of mystery, doesn't it? This what-you-may-call-it fellow—you know, this English fellow—"

"Sherlock Holmes," somebody said. There was a weak titter around the table.

Alesworth sat down again. Jaff Montgomery passed the letter on to Driscoll and turned his hard-lined face back to the others.

"I'll be the only one to know where the money's hidden," said Peter Alesworth, "except for the writer of the letter. Tomorrow night we are each to visit the billiard room alone, one at a time, in the dark. I'm supposed to go in last. Well, I take it that when I go in, the envelope full of money will be gone." His plump lips worked soundlessly for a moment. "Unless," he added, "I wrote this letter myself."

Montgomery's eyes held hard and angrily against Alesworth. "You could have."

"Yes, I could, couldn't I?"

John Britton said, "I could have, too. Any one of us could have written that letter. I guess whoever did it wanted to help— I mean— But I don't like the idea of employing a hired killer! Of course it *is* a good dodge: no one will have anything to do with the hiring, except the unknown party. We'll all have a clean bill of health . . . I don't like to think of this. . . ."

Probably none of the rest did, either; but Alesworth

voiced the feeling of all when he said quietly, "John, you've got to think of it. This is war."

On the next evening at approximately the same hour, the private supper room of the Stockmen's Club held the same group of men; but drawn supposedly by the magnet of poker rather than food. A circular green-baize table was already prepared with chips in the troughs, and the men played stud wearily in their shirt-sleeves, until finally Jaff Montgomery suggested that they might as well get to the business at hand.

The twelve thousand dollars in cash, including Alesworth's own two-thousand-dollar contribution, had been turned over to Alesworth and sealed in a heavy manila envelope. Most of the bills were of one-thousand-dollar denomination; the wad was thus not a large one.

At Montgomery's suggestion, the men played out the last hand of stud, and then locked both doors. The outer door of the billiard room had already been locked. They stood about, self-consciously tense, and some of them were grinning foolishly as Alesworth took the envelope and disappeared into the darkness of the billiard room.

He closed the door and walked deliberately to the pool table, finding his way more by familiarity than by sight. From outside a faint light creased through shutters and touched the thick staves of cues in their rack. They looked like slender pipes of the tiniest pipe-organ in the world, Alesworth thought. He stood against the solid bulk of the pocket-billiard table, and doubled the thick limpness of the envelope with which the death of certain inhabitants of the region might be bought.

34

After a few minutes he came out into the chamber where the others waited, and signalled that it was all right to go ahead; he had concealed the money in the place where he had been instructed to hide it, he said.

One after another, in the order named, Driscoll, Montgomery, Britton, Springstun and Webb retreated to the billiard room, and emerged after a brief interval.

"Webb's the last—except for you," came Britton's sharp voice. "Go ahead, Ales."

Alesworth revisited the darkness, and with him (except for the mutter of assassinations to come—the voiceless murmuring, the silent and imagined outcry of the hurt and the bereaved) there walked no sound except for the heavy click of billiard balls when he touched them. In darkness, he sent two of the balls rolling about the table . . . behind him, as he returned toward the closed door, he heard the balls wander . . . he heard their secret little thuddings against the beveled cushions . . . and strangely they never struck one another before they ceased their polished motion.

With a supreme exultation of relief, Peter Alesworth came out and slammed the door. The others watched him: five faces all severe in their wondering and doubt.

Alesworth got out his handkerchief and mopped his head again, and perceived that to others his bald head must look like a swollen ivory cue-ball.

"Was the money gone?" Montgomery demanded.

"It was in the left pocket of the pool table: the northeast corner pocket, under four balls I pushed down on top of the envelope. It was there, and now it's gone. I'm glad that's over."

John Britton may have muttered a prayer; it rather sounded like it. He exclaimed fervently, "So am I!" He had expressed frequently a congenital distaste for violence, and often he fired cow-hands merely because they got into a tussle.

Jaff Montgomery questioned Alesworth again: "So now you think it's one of us five?"

"Has to be."

"Unless it was you all the time."

Old Springstun cried, "Tut-tut, boys! That won't do any good." Then, "Suppose Bus Crow doesn't want to take the job?"

"The writer of that letter seemed to think he could be persuaded," Alesworth replied.

"How?" Springstun wanted to know.

"Oh, I suppose he might be put in the mood." Alesworth meditated about it, and heartily seconded the motion made by Driscoll to ring for drinks. He speculated aloud, "What does a young man think about out in this country, come Saturday night?"

Four

Mattie MacLaird was twenty-eight years old: a blonde woman with hard blue eyes, a loose and tender mouth, a round chin. She pretended to be twenty-five, and tried to give an impression of youth even greener than that.

At heart she was intrinsically too amiable to become predatory in any way, although if unprincipled she might have been a harpy of the cruelest sort. She could have gone about wheedling money from drunks, marrying foolish, lonely old cattlemen—or promising to marry them, and fleecing them in the process. The opportunity for such selfishness occurred commonly in her life.

She had loved without restraint on some occasions. With that persistent misfortune of the over-generous female, she had awarded her favors to a variety of inelegant scamps who brought her only woe. These miseries were unmentioned now; if Mattie had had a love affair since coming to Pearl City thirteen months earlier, no one knew about it.

She was a seamstress of sorts, and also gave a concert each Saturday night at the Glad Hand saloon. She was paid ten dollars for her minstrelsy by the cautious Ole

Paulson; but on busy evenings the tips and honoraria brought in a great deal more money than that. Nothing made Mattie happier than to have a heavy fold of greenbacks in her polished reticule: not for what she might do for herself, but because of the gifts she could award, the endowments she could make.

There was an ailing father back in Kansas City. She sent him money when she had it, and cheering little notes on any and all occasions. There were two little-girl cousins in Iowa, and these scrawny prairie-dwellers could thank Mattie for the hair-ribbons and dress-goods and buttons she sent.

She enjoyed too, the moments of casual philanthropy when Paulson was about to order some feckless old drifter flung out of the restaurant adjoining the bar, because he had not paid for his supper, and Mattie could signal firmly that she would pay the check.

Strangers in the town might mistake her for a prosti-tute—and sometimes did, to their eventful discomfiture. For the Saturday night song-fests, Mattie colored her cheeks and put choice red upon her lips. She had several items of glaring jewelry, and loved to bedizen her smooth arms with bracelets. But her hail-fellow-well-met air endeared her to the regulars at the Glad Hand even more than it encouraged unwelcome attentions from strangers, and won her a protection along with it.

Mattie did not live upstairs over the saloon, though she kept a little dressing-room there. Her bed, neat and unsullied, was made fresh for her night after night at the home of old Mrs. Ermels, a railroad widow. From

38

the Ermels cottage Mattie MacLaird marched briskly to the Methodist church each Sunday morning: not in a manner of pretense, but because she had been reared a Methodist and believed that this was the right thing for her to do.

There were cluckings from certain old hens who bristled their feathers in disdain. They manifested a moral contempt which in many cases concealed those universal secret weaknesses: jealousy, and the desire for emulation.

These women said that it was immoral for Mattie MacLaird to sing at the Glad Hand, to ruffle the hair and stroke the shoulders of a whiskey-bibbing audience, as she often did when she was in the mood. When her pathetic charities were brought to their attention, they disclaimed the fact, or attributed a loathsome motive. But such women occasioned little unhappiness for Mattie MacLaird by their attitude; she rather enjoyed, in her brassy way, being the subject of attentive gossip; her inner life was lonely, her loves now vicarious.

She stood on the stairway landing at the rear of the saloon. It was a few minutes after ten o'clock when Mattie formally began her concert. Art Schaub, a printer who loved to play the piano and performed thereon with some skill, was engaged for these musicales for a five-dollar fee; and many other nights he merely trailed into the saloon and sat down and played for nothing, because the Glad Hand piano was the only instrument available to him in town. Art had never played regularly in public and for a fee, until he became

Mattie's accompanist; but he enjoyed dearly all the claptrap of showmanship. He stopped Mattie whenever he met her on the street in order to draw her aside and, in his gushing, girlish voice, discuss remarkable plans, unheard-of crescendos and pianissimos, kerosene lamps turned quickly low, perhaps a blue-shaded light on the piano . . . fantastic weldings of their mutual talent to produce operatic effects never glimpsed before.

Mattie regarded Art Schaub as little better than an effeminate idiot, but she was always affectionate in her manner toward him; and, too, he was the only piano player at hand. She could play fairly well to accompany herself, and had done so when she began her singing career in Pearl City; but in Denver she had learned that the prettily-garbed artiste who roams flirtatiously among the population while she sings, will gather in a great many more tips than she who remains rooted to the piano-stool.

> Two little girls in blue, boys,
> Two little girls in blue,
> They were sisters, we were brothers,
> We learned to love the two—

Originally, Art had persuaded her to appear in a bright blue gown, and she had made such a dress for herself, despite the fact that she would be one little girl in blue, and not two. She had emerged from the doorway at the top of the stairs, singing poignantly and amidst thrilling applause; but within fifteen minutes a blundering roisterer upset a glass of Cuban punch down the front of Mattie's dress. She could not repair the damage properly herself, and there were no French cleaners in Pearl City. So Mattie dyed the dress black, toiling with stick and wash-boiler above Mrs. Ermels' hot wood-stove, and perhaps no eye but that of a too-inquiring female would recognize that this draped evening gown had not always been a marvel of heavy black silk.

She still sang, "Two Little Girls in Blue" in opening and closing. The habitues recognized it as her hallmark, and always joined in the second chorus.

On this night Mattie cried the final plaintive tragedy, "But we have drifted apart," from the upper platform. Then she descended the stairway slowly, her patched slipper feeling over the crooked steps below and ahead, her best pink-lace petticoat revealed daringly below the draped slice in her skirt. Art Schaub spoke fresh and ominous chords; he leered and beckoned with his eyes and head, and Mattie began her résumé of a completely fictive incident in a completely fictive war . . . or was it the Civil War? She neither knew or cared, but she could remember well enough when the song was first published and sung, and she had been born in 1871.

While the shot and shell were flying
Upon the battlefield,
The boys in blue were fighting,
Their Country's flag to shield.
Came a cry above the battle.
"Look, boys, our flag is down!
Who'll volunteer to save it from disgrace?"

It was a busy Saturday. There were many cowboys and other ranch hands from the big outfits, and a stag dinner-party promulgated by a local lodge chapter offered its share of noise and expenditure. The big room had shuddered and swelled with laughter, with the lower mumble of people along the bar, with the exclamations of the card players and the chatter of the few young women who either dared public disapproval by allowing themselves to be escorted to such a place, or were so far gone into admitted iniquity that they did not care.

(They wore simple suits and dresses—not the decolletage of racy Western legend; they were not dressed as ballerinas. The clean-up of Pearl City had come long before, at the behest of stern women like Mrs. Peter Alesworth and Mrs. John Britton, urging ministers and town councilmen alike to the task. No longer was there a bawdy-house above-stairs: only the apartment where dwelt the Paulsons with Ole's bedridden mother-in-law —only the little mirrored room, once a cubicle of sin, where Mattie MacLaird now left her costumes hanging through the week, and where she applied her powder and her rouge.)

> ". . . Just break the news to Mother,
> And tell her that I love her. . . .
> Just kiss her dear sweet lips for me,
> And break the news to her."

Five

Buster Crow sat in a blackjack game at a large circular table at the rearmost corner of the room—that table farthest from the bar and stairway. The lodge brothers who had dined earlier were embroiled in two large sessions of stud poker. This smaller game at the corner table was the outgrowth of a meeting between the owner of an implement company and the proprietor of Pearl City's only establishment devoted to the sale of packaged liquors. These gentlemen were old friends and practiced a sturdy gambling rivalry. They had started dealing blackjack hands more or less for fun. Finally one of them put down a five-dollar bill; soon the game had grown both in numbers and in capital involved.

Crow had wandered close to watch. There were five men besides the two original participants now involved. After Crow had stood watching for some time, the implement dealer looked up and invited him to play. Crow shook his head.

He resented the puzzle which he presented. The story of his coming, of his brawl with the Stivers and other details of his first visit to the Glad Hand, had been talked widely around town before Saturday night.

43

Ordinarily Bus Crow would have welcomed such gossip; it was bound to be stretched wildly beyond the original fact, and thus enhance his reputation; but he wished that he could have entered Pearl City under more auspicious financial circumstances.

He had only fifty-six dollars to his name besides his horse and a few small personal belongings; also he was in debt. He had returned from Cuba with a good-sized bankroll, but had lost a wallet containing the largest share of his capital—had lost it either on the train or else it had been stolen by a pickpocket. This latter possibility annoyed him particularly and seemed wholly plausible . . . he had walked constantly in crowds, he had been jostled.

Then there was a delayed reaction from tropical fever; he lay violently ill several times in recurrent four-week cycles. A doctor in St. Louis finally offered a kill-or-cure panacea. It seemed to have cured, not killed, but Crow still kept his fingers crossed figuratively. He dreaded the ghastly onslaught of the ailment which might return again to plague him: the burning high temperatures, the sudden collapse into ague—when he shivered so hard that his bed clattered through frame and springs, when with shaking hands he piled on every cover in the room, and even tried to wrap himself with loose rugs from the floor.

The fever would in fact not return, but he could not know this. He was weakened by the mere worry of the thing.

From boyhood he had stalked the world as a killer,

44

delighting in the thought of the trade he practiced: sometimes within the law, sometimes outside it. There was nothing he hated more than a man cowardly in weakness. He held the horrid thought that his own progressive physical weakness would make him cowardly; and yet he recognized that he might suffer even more from a feeling of financial impotence in this increasingly complex commercialistic world.

He was broke; he didn't like to think of it; his nearly-congenital bitterness and assumed unruly swagger were more apparent as a result.

It was well enough for the blabbing mouths of Pearl City to recite the advent of Bus Crow in the townspeople's midst, but what would they be saying about his shabby clothing? Would they assume that such garb was only the careless attitude of a man who could provide expensively for himself, and deliberately chose not to do so? Crow was too much of a realist to believe that. Thus he sulked as he watched the game.

Betting did not assume monumental proportions: five dollars seemed the standard, though no limit was set, and some of the later participants were wagering a cautious one or two dollars at a time. . . . Twenty-five dollars: he might risk that much and see how his luck ran.

Crow moved around behind the liquor-store man who was dealing, and observed his manner of play and the value of the cards that fell to him whenever there was a chance to steal a peek at them. This dealer at least was not especially wise or lucky, and he played a palpably honest game. These people were friends and neighbors of each other: there was no chance for anyone to be taken to a professional fleecing.

When one of the men moved out of the game, Buster accepted a second invitation to join in. Luck ran fairly toward him for a time, and when Mattie came down the stairs he had expanded his original twenty-five dollar stake to fifty-five dollars. In fact he had been considering asking about the limit, wondering if a single bet of twenty-five dollars would be allowed. If he got twin picture cards and split them, or if he went down for double and won. . . .

Crow resented the interruption brought by Mattie. Men talked about her: there was a slightly-obscene jest, a whispered confession of ambition toward her, but that was all. Mainly the men spoke of Mattie in good-natured and friendly terms.

She was, it appeared, a local institution, and they halted their game to cheer for "Two Little Girls in Blue," and to watch what they considered to be her amusing behavior as she wandered at last through the crowded room, singing "Break the News to Mother." On "break the news," she would clasp her hands lightly against one man's head; on "tell her that I love her," she would be hugging some old goat. The latter phrases of the chorus offered each their opportunity for pantomime.

When Mattie came to "kiss her dear sweet lips for me," she halted behind Sheriff Ballantine who sat with a crony playing cribbage for low stakes, and she implanted a warm kiss on the pink top of the old man's head. People roared with appreciation, then quieted again as the woman sang her way into the second chorus.

The dealer in Bus Crow's game did not offer fresh cards. He sat with others watching in amusement Mattie MacLaird's approach, and was delighted when she offered a salutation to him as she roved around the table. Bus Crow had to watch perforce; there was nothing else he could do.

She was one of the town girls, he supposed, or maybe a professional associated with this very restaurant and saloon: a call-girl for the out-of-towners, and perhaps also well-patronized by Pearl City folks. Yet even he, resenting women because of the power which they could in time exert against a man—even he could find a strength and flavor in this girl's appearance not common to other prostitutes of her supposed kind.

She was moving in behind him now, between Bus Crow and the old buffet in the corner where empty bottles stood amid white rings on the badly-varnished wood, and where the gilt handles of the drawers were chipped and broken.

She postured closer and closer; she let her arm stray along the shoulders of the man two places away from Bus. Now she was nearer, she stroked the shoulder of the man next to him. Mattie offered no kiss as she had done before, but when she sang the final line, "And break the news to her," she had come in to slide both arms around Bus Crow, bending behind him, holding her face close to his ear.

He sat rigidly, glaring straight ahead. He hoped to give the impression that the touch of this woman was completely repugnant to him; yet already he felt himself yielding to the odor of face powder, to the cheap sweet perfume she had touched upon her body, to the feel and rustle and odor of her very gown.

He could not believe it . . . yet she was whispering to him now, her low voice hidden from all other ears by the applause and alcoholic cheers that resounded.

She said, "Meet me outside. Out in back by the horse-trough. It's important."

Mattie strolled away. Crow sat wondering about her and about the message she had given. He still scarcely believed his ears. This was like something in a dime novel, or in lurid theatricals he had witnessed. *Meet me outside.* Was she joking? Who did she think he was, anyway—or, in fact, did she know who he was?

He lifted his cloudy gaze from the two fresh cards that had just flipped toward him, and looked to see whether Mattie was observing him now, and whether he could obtain any clue from her attitude. But she was only laughing, her arm lying across the big shoulder of the fat man who sat next on Bus Crow's right, and the fat man was squeezing her hand and talking about how he would take Mattie for a ride in his brand-new buggy, but he was afraid of what his wife would do to him when he got home.

Sheriff Ballantine made an unsteady path among the tables, and came floundering up to the group. He offered an oblong box of candy, ornate with a bow of red ribbon and silver paper on which the price-tag still flared.

Ballantine cried, "Here you are, Mattie. All for you!

48

Just paid Ole five dollars for it. It ain't none too good for you."

"Oh, thank you, Sheriff."

"It's chocolates, Mattie—lemon creams. Now you sing another song."

Mattie was unfastening the ribbon and opening the box, lifting the lid. "In just a few minutes I will, Sheriff. Let's everybody have some," and she began passing the candy around the table.

Under the charm of her generosity, most of the men helped themselves; the fat man took three pieces, but Bus Crow ignored the box when it was passed in front of him.

"Sing 'Lily Dale,' Mattie. Go on, sing 'Lily.' Or maybe 'Goodbye Dolly Gray,' ... what's that one about the little dolls?"

"'The Two Marionettes'?" asked Mattie. "Well, I'll sing something, Sheriff, and you were awfully sweet to give me the candy. I'll have some later. You know—not while I'm singing—"

She left the box on the big table between Bus and the man on his left, and Crow felt rather than saw that her eyes touched curiously across his face before she was gone.

He hit a twelve and lost with a jack. He could hear her words again, whispering close to him, "Out in back by the horse-trough." She must mean that open space off the little alley in front of the door of Stiver's livery stable, but why he should go he didn't know. Still, she had exerted some attraction not commonly the property of women you met in a saloon or heard singing there.

So Crow stood up, counted his money and said, as several of the players looked at him, "Be back in a minute." He went through a rear door, down a dirty hall, past the closed-up smelly kitchen and into darkness of the outside world. Mattie MacLaird was waiting for him.

Six

He heard first of all a steady trickling of water and his mouth hardened in distaste. There was a horse-trough, surely enough, in the open trampled area. Hot stars gave a good deal of light, though the first flake of the moon had sunk down and vanished. There were lanterns burning in night offices of the livery barn, and other bits of light shone from the Glad Hand behind Bus Crow. Mattie was revealed sharply.

She stood motionless as Crow walked slowly up to her, his boots crunching across the wheel-ruts.

"Well?" he asked.

He saw her pale hand rise to brush the fluffy hair back from her forehead. "It's nice out here, isn't it?"

"What do you want?"

"You're Buster Crow, aren't you?"

"Yes. What's your name?"

"Mattie. Mattie MacLaird." The woman tittered. "I thought everybody knew who I was—I mean in Pearl City."

"I haven't been around here very long."

"I know you haven't. But people will talk. You're

looking for a job, aren't you? And you claim to have killed sixty-seven men. . . ."

He didn't like the way she said that. "What do you mean—claim?"

The woman's low voice stole on in a kind of singsong. "You're living in Room Six over at the Continental. Well, you're supposed to go up to Room Twenty-seven on the second floor at one o'clock tonight."

Not only was Crow infuriated by the calm insouciance in which she tried to fold her nervousness, but he did not like to be ordered 'round.

He gave his grudging laugh. "Room Twenty-seven. If I go, who'll I find? You?"

In satiny rustle she draw away from him. The insult had hurt her. "Bus Crow," she said, "you're a mean man, aren't you?"

"How did you guess?"

All the time that water was bending itself from the spout of the horse-trough, leaning upon the unseen surface beneath . . . a shapeless, loose substance of sound coming down, striking gently, bubbling . . . a million horrid voices spoke amid its gurgles . . . and Bus Crow thought of a loose faucet in the wash-room at the Continental: already he hated to enter that wash-room because of a whimpering he recognized in the liquid flow. He thought of the unclosed beer-tap, the afternoon before; and how, mercifully, in response to irate demand, Ole Paulson's hand had pressed the instrument of torture and brought a hasty peace once more.

But there lived other moisture, gushing in pallid

thinness, in broken drip-drip-drip through all the years behind. And there were other rages even more brutish than the viciousness that rose now within him.

The woman Mattie: she represented a torture, because there was the smell and sound of satisfaction about her, the dance of pleats and laces girding her body: the things he loved and from which he fled assiduously, because he must never allow himself to be ensnared and thus turned vulnerable.

The passion to which he admitted was braided with the need to inflict a physical cruelty. He recognized and yielded to this wickedness as the majority of men would never do—no matter how strongly they might feel the desire to crush and pummel a certain woman— to bruise her wide-flung arms, to form in symbol a greedy mutilation of the act of love.

Above the chirping water talk, darkness welcomed suddenly a rustle and a gasp, the sound of a slight struggle, the sound of a slap.

Mattie was backing away from Bus Crow, holding her hand against her mouth, staring up at the man with wide eyes.

"Why," she sobbed, "you—you— You like to hurt people, don't you?"

In those few seconds she had become frightened; through her entire experience she had never met anyone like this man.

She cried softly, "Yes, you kiss. But you're not friendly when you kiss. I don't like you!"

The trough trickled smugly beside them; a fresh awareness of it kept the fury in Crow's voice.

53

"I don't like you, either. What have you got up your sleeve? Why did you get me to come out here—out by this—this running water?"

He advanced again, the woman gave ground. She was still pressing the back of her hand against her throbbing lip. Could she sing again this night? . . . she wondered frantically.

"All right," she said over and over. "All right, I did it. I did it. I *told you!*" Then her back was against the trough, she could retreat no farther.

"Who hired you? Who gave you that yarn about Room Twenty-seven at the Continental?"

"I don't know."

"Yes, you do."

"It's the actual truth: I don't know. I went into my dressing room tonight and there was a letter right against the mirror and—and some money in it. The letter told me to tell you, and— I don't know who sent it, or how. I don't know who put it there—"

And when he waited before her silent, hulking, she asked weakly, "What are you going to do about it?"

He seemed pondering even as she asked him. "I don't know. Tell you, though: you sing another song, come around to the table when you do, and I'll give you my answer."

Crow turned abruptly and went away, irritable and confused. He was torn between his impulse to possess this woman for his own joy, and his even stronger desire to crush and tear her body in some ugly fashion. She represented a force against which he had battled since

he was small: no remembered creed or cult, no identi-
fiable group—only the world of men and women at
large—the vast multitude of breathing, talking humans
whom he despised relentlessly and whom he would kill
if he could.

Seven

For a few more hands in the card game Bus Crow see-sawed back and forth.

Then he received a serious blow: he split queens, stayed with an eighteen on one and a nineteen on the other, and the dealer hit sixteen with a five. Thus Crow lost twenty dollars and began his descent into a deeper penury.

The loathing which he felt for the others in the game, for himself, and for Mattie MacLaird (when once more she came into the room to sing) was sharpened into action when he dropped a silver dollar on the floor. The coin rolled under the edge of the old buffet behind him. Crow left his chair with an unspoken curse. It was bad luck dropping that coin, and he had to go down on one knee in order to retrieve the dollar.

Then he saw something else: a rectangular object placed motionless in those shadows by hands other than his . . . Bus Crow grinned within his raw, flayed soul. He took up the dollar and the other thing as well, and kept it concealed on his lap for a time.

Mattie began her encore. "There'll Be a Hot Time," and once more she was drifting from table to table. She strewed pretended caresses along her way to the corner of the room where sat Bus Crow, his winnings

gone and his meager, bankroll sicker by some thirty-
five dollars.

> When you hear
> Them bells go ting-a-ling,
> All join hands
> And how sweetly we will sing—

She came round the table; the wall behind her was
a sounding-board; her firm voice, colorful but mainly
untutored, swept out across the room. The younger
men especially were pleased by the words she sang—
even more pleased, perhaps, than by her tactics of
endearment among them. Some had served in the
Philippines or in Cuba. The version of the song which
Mattie now sang had been cried from windows of hot
wooden coaches when the troops rolled to rendezvous
in the South. They listened to the words; they imagined
the sergeants' orders being shouted again. . . .

The smudge of a slight bruise was puffing already on
her upper lip beneath the red painted there, as Mattie
swayed toward Bus Crow.

He pulled back his chair; then, with a gesture of
extreme courtesy (ludicrous, in the manner of one
unaccustomed to performing any courtesies at all)
Crow lifted the box of candy, took off the lid, and
offered chocolates to Mattie MacLaird.

> There'll be a hot time
> In Cuba tonight, Sagasta—

On the word "Sagasta" her hand went into the box
among the frilled papers.

Shrill, decisive, the pop of a snapping mouse-trap

terminated the song and wrung a little scream from Mattie. She stood shaking her fingers on which the trap had clamped, trying to work the thing loose.

There was momentary silence in the roomful of men who watched her, than a growing murmur of outrage. But high over that murmur rose the roar of Buster Crow.

He was rocking back and forth in his chair, surrendered completely to the merriment that welled within him. On either side of him men leaped to their feet; the fat fellow who had been sitting on Crow's right, now held Mattie's quivering arm while other hands disengaged the mouse-trap.

Face after face, the men's glances turned away from the victim of the prank and fried in unholy disgust against the man who had played it.

Bus Crow's laugh diminished in volume, his chuckles sought a lower octave. Abruptly they went into his throat—deeper and deeper, as if a new and even more horrid emotion were stifling them.

He had left off laughing, and slowly he rose to his feet. His right hand pushed aside the skirts of the old brown coat, and his thumb was hooked over the gun-belt near the butt of his revolver. Again tortured in that unspoken agony of pleading, his eyes went over the men with whom he had been playing cards, and seemed to pass through them with the speed of stones hurled through a window-pane, and seemed splintering among people at other tables.

He gave them his question, flat and sharp. "That was funny, wasn't it?"

58

No one spoke a word.

"I say it's funny. . . . Laugh! Why don't you laugh? All of you—*laugh.*"

They knew his reputation; they had heard of his killings in the Green River country, the gun fights at Cheyenne, the one-man massacre he perpetrated near Grand Lake. They knew that he was demoniacal in his addiction to the gun.

. . . The face of the weakest and most frightened man (he was the liquor-store proprietor) began to twist and shiver. He broke into a tremulous giggle—a weak and horrid sound—and turned fearfully to look at the man next him.

Still Buster Crow stood with coat thrust back, waiting for his demand to be obeyed. By this time his fingers had moved wholly over the revolver butt. Some said later that he drew the weapon from its holster; others said that he didn't even touch the gun; no one could remember for a certainty.

Their eyes were drawn to his; they saw the ardent savagery of his face; they did not watch what he did with his hand, or with the metal menace he stood ready to control. . . . They were all laughing, though Mattie MacLaird had turned away to hide her face. The awful *ho-ho-ho* (a manufactured sound more starkly hideous than any screaming) rose up in a steady chant.

Crow turned away from the table and walked directly across the room, putting on his flat black hat as he went. The slatted twin doors swung apart when his elbow touched them, they rubbed together when he had gone, and the laughter went dead behind him.

Eight

He walked around town for nearly an hour, trying to decide what to do. He could only guess at what might result if he were to act upon the summons relayed by Mattie, and visit Room Twenty-seven at the Continental Hotel at one o'clock. The message had the impact of a command, and never did Buster Crow wish to be commanded.

He could not imagine who might have originated the plan, nor could he understand the purpose behind it. There were people in other regions not too far removed from Pearl City who would cheerfully slaughter Bus Crow in revenge for some bereavement or other hurt they had suffered at his hands, yet none of them dared risk meeting him in a stand-up fight.

Ordinarily Crow felt himself invulnerable, but it seemed silly to risk a possible knifing or some other kind of treachery, by going to a strange hotel room in such devious fashion.

Two or three times he stepped into darkness among the shadows, watching carefully to observe whether or not he was being followed. He found no evidence that anyone was trailing him, even though his wanderings

60

carried him to lonely regions along the railroad tracks. Finally he returned to Center Street and its few lights, and went directly toward the pale bulk, the long frame box of the Continental House.

His own room, Number Six, was near the rear on the ground floor. On the opposite side of the hotel, another building bulked close; but on this north side there was empty space outside his room. Bus held his door ajar before he entered, letting the draught wash stagnant air from the dark chamber. Then he entered, closed the door and locked it, and felt his way to the dresser, fumbling for a lamp. He struck a match, touched its flame to the lamp-wick, and replaced the glass chimney.

He hated the poverty of this little pen, and hated the testimony of his retreating fortunes evidenced by the battered valise and the few toilet articles on the dresser top. But he had half a bottle of whiskey left. He drank thirstily. He shuddered and paused . . . the whiskey cough was with him again, as it had been before he went to the war.

He took off his suit-coat and hat, threw his coat on the bed and spun his hat to the iron post nearest him. He held a few superstitions: a hat upon a bed was one of them. He unbuckled the weight of his gun-belt and hung belt and holster over the post. Another drink . . . what did he have left? Only sixteen dollars. . . .

Standing before the mirror to drink once more, and seeing himself tousled and mighty, baleful as always, hating himself in the cracked mirror's gleam, he saw more than himself. He saw the man in the checkered

61

shirt who disarranged the curtain of a makeshift wardrobe at the other end of the room and descended noiselessly upon Bus Crow, revolver ready and pointed.

At first it seemed an illusion . . . but the man was coming closer; he could fire before Bus might ever reach the gun he had discarded a moment before.

There was nothing to do but to put his hands above his head.

The man was Crashaw, Jaff Montgomery's employee, but Crow did not know that. Vaguely he remembered having seen Crashaw in the Glad Hand that night; he was one of many.

"Your door was locked but your window wasn't."

"Had to wait until I took off my gun, didn't you?"

"I wasn't taking any chances."

"What do you want—money? I haven't got any."

Crashaw grinned through the lamplight. "So they cleaned you in that blackjack game?"

Crow said, "I didn't have much for them to clean. What are you trying to do—trying to be the man who killed the man who killed the man—?"

"Somebody sent me."

"Same trick as with the girl. . . ."

Crashaw told him, "I don't know anything about that. I'm just handing a message on to you. They want you to go up to Room Twenty-seven. But go quiet."

"Who's they?"

"I don't know. There'll be a little table pulled in front of the door going to Room Twenty-eight. You sit down at that table and put your hands on top."

62

Bus Crow cried from the depths of perplexity, "What the hell's this all about, anyway?"

"Don't ask me—I was hired in the dark. I got in some trouble a while back and had to pay a big fine; lucky I wasn't fired. Money talks good to me: this was a fifty-dollar bill, and I liked what it said. You go up there and there'll be a curtain behind that table. Don't touch that curtain, understand? Don't—touch—the curtain."

"Why not?"

"That I can't tell you, mister. Just don't touch it." He moved the muzzle of his gun slightly—very slightly indeed—and with a sidewise motion of his head he indicated the door. "Come on."

Crow stepped ahead of Crashaw into the kerosene-smelling light and shadow of the hallway. He thought momentarily of wheeling on his captor and struggling for possession of the revolver. He was bigger than this intruder, but there was a nasty risk involved; Crashaw wisely kept his distance as they moved toward the stairs. There were no other hotel guests in sight, although Bus could hear feet pounding distantly on the front stairway near the office, he could hear someone laughing.

He went slowly up the rear stairway, Crashaw following. In the upper hall, opposite the door of Room Twenty-seven which was on the south side of the building, Bus Crow turned to look at the man behind him, but Crashaw only motioned again with his gun.

Crow turned the knob of the door; it was unlocked. The door swung easily, and he went inside; he did not

63

know what he might find in the room, but by this time he did not care particularly. He was wearied by the fever which had pained and weakened him during the months before; he was wearied by his poorness, embittered by his lack of sense of direction. But he hated the thought of a fate which might come to him in such ignominy, and nerved himself for a tussle to avoid it.

No one seemed waiting in this place after he had closed the door. As Crashaw had described, a little table was drawn up against a curtained doorway; there was a chair placed ready and a student lamp on the table.

Bus Crow approached the table gingerly. He halted once and looked around into the shadows on either side, but he could see nothing.

He seated himself and spread his hands on the table top as he had been ordered to do. Faded calico curtains of the doorway were motionless beyond him; but there was a slight aperture; a ribbon of blackness two or three inches wide.

A man spoke from the distance beyond.

"Don't touch the curtains. Is that understood?"

The voice was tinny and sepulchral: it had an unearthly resonance about it.

Crow sat staring before him. "Your voice is funny," he said. "What's the matter with it?"

"I'm talking into a large tin pail, to disguise my voice."

"What's to stop me from reaching over and tearing that curtain down?"

"A sawed-off shotgun. It's lying here, aimed directly at you."

Bus Crow settled back in his chair. "Go ahead and talk."

"Crow, we've got a job for you."

"Who's 'we'?"

"Some of the big ranchers hereabouts. We want you to represent us."

He thought, *By God, this does sound like money.* He felt that his ears were lifting, opening and pointing like the ears of an alert dog.

"How do I represent you?"

The voice said, "You will be given a list of names. You are to invite those men to leave the country."

"Well, what if they don't want to leave?"

"We thought you'd know what to do about that. You will get six hundred dollars for each man."

And now he could see the six hundred dollars: high happy cylinders stacked up like coinage in a mint, the polished silver shafts rising metallic to delight him.

"That's a lot of money. Why bother to warn them, anyway? Why don't I just go out and shoot them?"

The other man—the low, tinny echoing tone—told him distinctly, "If you don't warn them, we will. We don't want murder—we want to hire a police force, and you're it. Here's the situation, Crow: we've had our beef slaughtered, calves branded, cattle stolen, fences going up. We've had all we can stand. We were here first, brother, and we intend to stay. If we stay, those rustlers—those movers—they've got to go."

Movers, the man had said, and Crow saw them clearly now . . . mended wagon with the strained axle and ragged canvas top, the people who rode there, the people who followed. . . .

He said in a whisper, hypnotized into recollection by the most fiendish imagining, "Movers, mister? I hate movers. They travel in wagons—they've got kids— mean kids. Movers shot— They shot—"

"Who did they shoot?"

Bus Crow lifted his hands slightly, and the curtains before him twitched in warning. He dropped his palms back upon the table with a sound. "Six hundred apiece. I'll do it! I've got a modified Mannlicher—got it in Tampa. Nobody around here has ever seen a gun to beat it."

"What's so good about that?"

"Got a telescopic sight—takes an eight millimeter cartridge—"

"What?"

"That's about three-one-five caliber. It can reach as far as you can see a man—" Crow was babbling momentarily in almost hysterical enthusiasm. "Don't worry! The gun's in my plunder. I've got a trunk in storage— stored in Denver—and I'll get it."

The man behind the curtain seemed considering this, perhaps wondering just how this strange European rifle could affect the case, but he asked no more about it.

"Open that drawer in front of you," he said, and Crow did open the drawer, although the cheap wood had swelled—the drawer gripped tightly, and he had to waggle it from side to side.

66

"See that envelope? It's got the names of the first three men. Also six hundred dollars in cash."

"Why don't you give me the whole list of men all at once?"

"Don't worry—you'll get more names as you need them, also more money. We want to see how you do on this first job, that's all."

Bus Crow tore open the plain brown envelope; he took out a generous fold of currency, and that was good to see. He felt busy blood flowing anew through his empty veins; he achieved a power and a purpose merely from holding that money.

He counted the bills: hundreds, fifties, five twenties. He fondled each bill in the counting. He put the money in his pocket, and then unfolded the slip of paper.

There were three names; they meant nothing in particular to him; they were merely names which he had never heard before. But he would find the men. He had always found them.

Beyond the curtains, in the darkness of Room Twenty-eight, there had sounded a thump and scraping as Bus Crow counted the money. Now, lifting his eyes to the motionless calico folds before him, Crow rose with stealthy speed. He stepped around to one side of the doorway, then with a quick jerk he ripped the curtains down. Nothing happened; no gun blast.

Another table, similar to the one at which he had sat, was just beyond the doorway; another chair was there, too, and an empty tin pail. No shotgun.

The room was illuminated only by the lamp in Room

Twenty-seven, and by the vaguest light from outside. Through dimness Crow could see that the hall door was closed.

He shoved the tables aside and plunged across Room Twenty-eight. He tried the hall door: it was locked. He turned and went rapidly toward the window, blundering into furniture on the way and overturning a chair. As he reached the open window he heard remotely the sound of a man hastening down a flight of stairs. He leaned far out across the sill through midnight gloom.

There was a flat roof adjacent—a one-story building next to the hotel . . . a harness shop in that building, Crow remembered. But the wide platform of the roof was empty, and now empty also was a flight of wooden stairs at the rear. The fugitive had vanished.

Crow knelt at the window ledge for a time. He could not resist the impulse to take the money out of his pocket again and rub it between his fingers. There was no one to watch him . . . no eye but the eyes of Heaven and the bats that may have wheeled above the town . . . he grinned as he might have smiled before a receptive audience. Now again he had a joy in life—the eternal beguiling joy which was always his, in life: the joy of making death.

Nine

The sign before the doorway read:

P. W. ALESWORTH CATTLE COMPANY
PEARL CITY OFFICE
THE BUSTED A

—and at the bottom was a representation of Alesworth's cattle brand—a capital A with parts of one of the sides missing.

Alesworth enjoyed this fancy: it told the history of his earlier failure to establish himself as a man of fortune (he had gone broke at the age of thirty-nine) —and by implication it recited his pride in the comeback he had made.

A roll-top desk in his private office at the rear of the little shack was littered with papers. Old receipts, letters long answered but never filed away: these crusted in a yellowish mat over the whole surface of the desk, on which the top was never drawn down and locked.

Alesworth squatted comfortably in his chair, heavy eyelids pressed nearly together, his pale mouth squeezing a wet cigar-stub.

"So you've already quit your job, have you?"

"Yes," said Mattie MacLaird. "I quit Saturday night."

She was seated close. She wore a neat gray suit with a nosegay of daisies from her landlady's garden pinned on the wide reveres of her jacket. Free of the exaggerated makeup she wore at the Glad Hand, there was now something both arresting and appealing about Mattie's face: a bright honesty shone there, though there was pain as well.

Alesworth asked, "Why did you quit, Mattie? You've been at the Glad Hand ever since you came to town. Just that, and a little dressmaking on the side, I guess."

The girl sighed and stirred restlessly in her chair. "Before I came here I had a job singing in Denver. . . . But something happened Saturday night. Maybe you heard.

"No, I—"

She played with the buttons of the one glove she had removed. "Oh, I guess I've been sick of the whole business for a long time. Maybe I didn't know it before. You know how it is—or you can guess. Singing, doing an act—even drinking and being friendly with the men—that's one thing. Getting hurt—that's something else."

"So you got hurt?" He had heard all about it on Sunday; he lied when he said he had not heard.

Mattie whispered, "Mr. Alesworth, you've got daughters of your own: I guess that's the reason I came to you. You've always seemed so friendly and— I just thought that maybe you'd know some place— I haven't got enough money to go very far, but I do want to get

70

out of that kind of environment. Something seemed to change inside me when I was—hurt."

Cattle had broken away from a herd that was being shipped, and several loose steers wandered through the street outside. Alesworth sat listening to the distant laughter and calling of townspeople, to the yells of cowboys who were rounding up the straying cattle. These sounds suggested to him the futility of Mattie Mac-Laird's search for other employment in a place like Pearl City.

He asked idly, "Ever done any typewriting or stenography stuff, or anything like that?"

Mattie shook her head. She fought to keep the alert and winning smile fastened to her face, though her heart was sinking. "No, the only thing I ever did before Denver—I guess you'll laugh—I was a country school-teacher. Maybe that sounds funny—an entertainer at a saloon, teaching school."

"Why didn't you keep on teaching school?"

"Oh, I thought I'd like to have a good time. Well, I had it. It wasn't such a good time."

The cattleman's gaze went over her again. Fundamentally he was direct and simple as to nature, and the possession of his daughters had warmed a kindliness within him. He disliked to admit that at times the devious cruelty of the world forced him to be devious and cruel himself, or at least he fancied it did.

"Mattie," he said, "you really put me in mind of something. You know, they need a schoolmarm over here in the Elk Run country. It doesn't pay much—maybe that's the reason they're always needing a teacher.

Five months out of last year they didn't have one. They'd send their kids to the schoolhouse at the drop of a hat, if a girl showed up who could really teach— or a man, either, for that matter."

"Mr. Alesworth, would they mind about me?"

He said cautiously, "Well, a few of the sanctimonious folks might hit the ceiling at the idea of—"

"I know what you mean."

He bustled into action; already he was digging beneath the layer of papers to find a blank sheet of stationery. "Maybe they could be persuaded. That is, just so long as you were careful what kind of songs you taught the kids."

Mattie bounced to her feet. Alesworth saw that there was moisture around her frizzly blonde hair-roots, and she was squeezing her glove into a pulp.

This girl was earnestly interested in doing what she said . . . the man felt a warmth creep within him as he recognized her truth, her warm heart.

"Do you really think they'd let me try?" Mattie cried.

He found a pen and began to write. "I'll give you a letter to a Mr. Bainbridge out there. It might do some good."

It did some good.

Ten

Carey Miller and his wife came back
from town with a week's groceries and
two spools of new wire in the wagon.
It did not affect them to think that the bulk of these
spoils had been purchased with money received from
beef which they had stolen, butchered, and sold to a
local shop. They had no conscience in the matter: they
fancied themselves in the role of little people defensive-
ly at war against immense, aggressive interests. But
for the first time they felt actual trepidation as they
read the note nailed securely on their front door.
They held it flat against the dry wind to read it.

Carey Miller. You have
two days in which to
sell out and leave.

Miller ripped the note off the door and tore it to
pieces. However, that night he slept with a double-
barreled shotgun loaded and leaning against the boards
beside the head of the bed. He carried the shotgun with
him whenever he moved abroad, and that was not

far. He merely fed his stock and did odd chores. He did not go down to the other end of the land he had claimed, to dig more postholes.

It was a Wednesday when he and Janet Miller found the note. Early Saturday morning, Miller opened his door, peered cautiously around, and came out carrying a wooden pail to the pump perhaps a hundred feet from the stoop of the shack. He lugged the shotgun in his left hand, and as he worked the handle of the pump he kept glancing in different directions. Carey Miller was nervously fearful, half-inclined after those days of strain and vigilance to obey the injunction of the warning and give up what he had already won.

The bucket was filled. The man lifted it off the spout and started up the slope toward his house. From behind and to one side there sounded the *whang* of a rifle shot. Carey Miller waved the bucket wildly: it flew far out from his hand, water and all, and the shotgun dropped beside him. Miller fell on his face, rolled half over on his back, and then lay motionless.

From inside the house Janet had cried her quick alarm as she heard the report of the rifle. She sped out of the doorway and ran toward her husband, running with pain and limping badly, for she had been troubled with phlebitis for years. Before she reached the body she halted and then backed off, cowering.

Bus Crow had risen from behind a heap of rocks inside the barbed wire fence; he held in his hands the Mannlicher rifle with which he had killed the homesteader. Crow could not be recognized by anyone. He wore a home-made black hood with eyeholes cut in it:

74

a hideous shroud that draped down to conceal much of his attire.

Janet Miller sank in collapse as Crow halted above the dead body, and stared at her through the hideous round-cut holes. He drew back the bolt of his rifle and deliberately ejected an empty cartridge. The metal tube struck against one of Miller's shoes and flipped into the dust alongside. It lay there glistening.

. . . Charley Bevin was alone when the assassin visited him; no one saw Buster Crow come or go. The note of warning was fastened on Bevin's door sometime during Saturday night. Although he did not learn of the murder of Miller until another twenty-four hours had passed, Bevin was reduced to an abject state from the very first. His dread intensified after he heard about Miller. . . . Bevin was a disheartened drunk of middle age, and this attempt at homesteading out in the long ranges south and east of Pearl City had been marked from its inception as the final desperate striving of a man eternally convinced that the cards were stacked against him.

But he did not leave his claim—not even when the shadows fell long on Tuesday, and he knew that his two days were gone. He had no relatives thereabouts (or anywhere else, for that matter); no place else to go; his entire capital had been sunk in the construction of a small dwelling and the fences surrounding it, and in the accumulation of a few sheep. He sat at a table piled with dirty dishes; he had a half-gallon jug of liquor beside him, and already he had emptied a broken-handled teacup three times when Bus Crow appeared.

75

Footsteps came across the darkening ground outside, then up on the wooden step. Bevin started to his
feet; he dropped his teacup. There was the creak of the
door being opened, the angry explosion of a weapon
fired within-doors . . . an explosion which Charley Bevin
never heard, for the hot bullet drilled his brain before
the sound could be registered there.

Blood flew, the face twisted . . . Bevin fell against
the table, upsetting the jug before he went to the
floor. Liquor trailed from the jug's mouth, but not for
long. There came the crash of another shot; the jug
flew to pieces; no more trickling; no more hateful and
persistent outpouring of the tuneful moisture which
Bus Crow despised and feared.

. . . Eleven head of cattle filed into the pen at Simon
Teal's place on a Friday. They were Herefords of a
scrubby variety, but Teal was proud of them. He was
mainly decent in his small business habits, and except
for a brief enterprise in a hair-branding scheme some
years earlier in western Nebraska, he had always pre-
served a scrupulous honesty. He had appropriated no
calves belonging to the big ranchers since he came to
Pearl County, nor had he slaughtered any cattle on the
open range.

The knowledge of his own probity sustained him
when that awful sheet of paper was first tacked upon
his porch post. Teal was a former cavalryman and could
shoot with a hand-gun; he kept a Colt's revolver showing prominently in the holster on his overalled hip.

He swung the wooden gate to admit his cattle, and
as he held the gate open, his right hand was closed

76

on the butt of his revolver. He was ready for any threat which might identify itself.

The last of the cows swung their tails past him. Simon Teal turned away to drag against the gate. The sharp note of the foreign rifle strummed. Unlike Bevin, he heard the explosion of the cartridge which killed him . . . he was conscious of the cattle crowding away from the gate as he toppled to his knees. First there was one thing to do . . . the enemy had come . . . he must draw his weapon. He did contrive to disengage the revolver from its holster, but then his curving fingers found only blackness . . . he thought that once again he heard his mother talking about wild-grape jelly, before all discernment fled away from him.

He lay doubled in the dust, nor felt the empty cartridge tossed out by a mechanism soon held above him—the casing that fell upon his body and glanced from the belt-buckle with a *clink*.

Simon Teal's cattle watched the killer approach and leave his mark. Two of them lifted their heads to blat stupidly.

Eleven

There were other cows in the nearby country, and some of them were in the Elk Run schoolhouse. Forever in one of the few colored illustrations of the *First Reader,* a pretty gold-and-white cow nuzzled her calf; and forever a little girl's eyes found delight in the spectacle . . . as delight dwelt in the candy tints of the illustrated flag, the purple of the grapes, the russet of the apple.

June Arden read slowly. There was tender breathing, a protracted speculation between each of the one-syllable words. She intoned: "The . . . cow . . . is . . . king . . . to . . . her . . . calf. . . ."

"No, dear," said Mattie MacLaird, "what is this word?" She held her finger on the page.

Mattie was squeezed in beside June at the end of a long bench where several other pupils were crowded. These were children of the first and second grades. Mattie felt more immediately drawn to little June Arden (a skinny five-year-old with ethereal gray eyes and a bleached gingham dress) than she felt to the others. She tried to be the perfect preceptress: fair in her judgments, sympathetic, but always in command. She tried never to reveal the kinship she might feel basically

78

for one child, and her native antagonism for another.

But she failed miserably where June Arden was concerned. In this tiny face and body were epitomized the frailty, the infant femininity which Mattie MacLaird longed to possess for herself. She had always wanted to have children. Her maternal inclination pulsated with nearly the fervor of the erotic appetite which by domination over body and spirit had at times brought her to grief.

This craving for amoral dalliance she had held in check during her months at Pearl City. She gave herself to charities and miscellaneous kindnesses even when the recipient was incapable of appreciating them. Now, at Elk Run, Mattie found a fuller substitution for the love acts she had ruled from her existence.

There was a sensation of joy achieved in merely regarding the bright, unformed faces of the children. She loved to slide her arm around the wiry shoulders of the most rascally boy; she found overpowering pleasure in sitting close to little June, in hearing the girl's nervous breathing as she approached the ordeal of recitation, in feeling the big eyes that stole up from the primer now and then to regard Mattie with awe and trust.

"No, dear," said Mattie again. " 'The cow is' —not *king*— that isn't a G. What am I to you?"

June Arden thought for a moment. Then she giggled, determined on the first joke she had ever attempted with her teacher. "Cross!" said the child explosively.

Mattie laughed. There was whispering going on

behind her; she turned to warn the boys. "Fred—Larry —that'll be enough whispering!" Then she turned back to the child, saying, "Come, now. That's a D."

June said happily, "Kind. The cow is *kind* to her calf."

There was a glory in this that Mattie MacLaird had never found when she minced on the stairway, singing, "Two Little Girls in Blue," saluted by a hundred men.

Late that afternoon, after her scholars were gone, Mattie stood behind her desk, sorting out the spelling and geography papers of the elder students to take home and correct during the evening. The interior of the little building was bleak, but already Mattie had attempted to brighten things up with photographs of McKinley and Leonard Wood and T. Roosevelt, a few gay pages cut from magazines, Rosa Bonheur animal prints taken off old calendars—things like that.

She was pleased with herself and with her job, though like every inhabitant of the region she felt serrated wings beating across the landscape . . . she did not think about them too much. She was immediately ambitious, and dreaming of joys and profits for the children of her flock, and of perceiving what improvements she might instigate before winter snows slashed the term to an end.

She was surprised to find herself visited by Gare Stiver and his son Willie, who rode up outside, dismounted and came shambling in across the doorstep. Gare pulled off his hat and nudged Willie to follow suit.

Mattie had not expected to find the livery stable

proprietor and his son wandering the Elk Run country. But Gare explained promptly that he had lost the stable—he couldn't pay the note for money he had borrowed—and he had pledged his barn and horses as security.

"My wife's brother staked me to some land up the valley here," he said ruefully. "The house isn't much, but I've got a few head of cattle. Mattie, I wanted to see about having Willie come to school."

Willie was no pleasant acquisition for any school, but Mattie did her best to offer a bright welcome. "We'll enjoy having you, Willie. You be on time Monday morning, bright and early." She added in an aside to the father, "You've got a lot of courage to start in ranching, the way things are."

Stiver played with a cracked glass inkwell-lid on the desk where he was sitting. "You mean all these killings? I don't know who'd want to bother me. I'm small fry."

Mattie folded her class papers into a large envelope, and in modest concealment behind her desk, began to unfasten the buttons of her divided riding skirt. "But all the men who've been killed seem to have been— small fry."

"I can't understand who's doing it. Somebody must be getting well paid."

She was ashamed at having opened such a subject. "Well, we'll all try to forget our troubles Saturday night," she told the unhappy man before her.

"You mean the doings here at the schoolhouse? We can't come. My wife says she hasn't got a dress fit to come in."

"That's nonsense," cried Mattie, instantly recoiling from the cheap, unprideful attitude manifest. "Nobody around here is rich; there'll be lots of old gowns at the Harvest Dance. I'm looking forward to it. I've never been to a Harvest Dance."

She took up her straw sailor hat and pinned it atop her blonde hair, as Stiver and his son followed her to the door.

"You're living with old Mr. Mason and his wife, aren't you?" the man said. "Guess we'd better ride along with you."

That, too, was silly, said Mattie again. The Mason house lay down the valley, not up, and it was only three miles.

"You can't tell," said Stiver darkly, as Mattie left him in the schoolyard and rode away. "All these killings," he was insisting again. "Somebody must be getting well paid. . . ."

Indeed somebody was getting well paid. That night there was a stout poker game at the Glad Hand saloon, and Buster Crow sat in the game, well-provided with chips. It was not a Saturday night: there was only a small crowd, and the game included five men through most of the evening—six men at the most. Backed by ample funds, Crow prospered. He had won more than seven hundred dollars when the game came to its close. Even then he lingered a while, cutting the deck with a Denver traveling man at five dollars a throw, and he sent Paulson behind the bar for the second quart of whiskey which he had purchased.

Old Sheriff Ballantine stood at the bar with two

other men, watching the transaction. He saw Bus Crow draw a roll from his pocket. He watched greedily as Crow pulled back the bills one by one; they were all of large denomination. Finally Bus carelessly picked up a five-dollar bill from the loose money in front of him and told Paulson to keep the change.

The old sheriff shook his head. He spoke in a low tone to the others, scarcely moving his mouth under its shaggy mustache.

"He's been winning all week, but not *that* much."

Forty minutes later, had the sheriff but known it, Buster was even richer. He stood in the lamplight of his hotel room, reading a letter discovered on the dresser, and there was a wad of fresh currency gripped in his hand as well.

". . . Good work on the last two cases," the letter read. "The additional twelve hundred dollars is enclosed as promised. Here are the next three names: Ed Nailey, Gus Bainbridge, Davis Arden. Payment will be made as soon as these matters have been attended to."

The letter offered a bit of warning before it closed. "One thing you had better watch: you are keeping too much to yourself, and suspicion may center on you."

Already Bus Crow could feel suspicion following him whenever he walked the streets, whenever he rode abroad, whenever he strode down halls of the Commercial House or through the doorway of the Glad Hand. Suspicion . . . people had been suspicious of him before. But the only conviction obtained was in their own minds —never in a court-room.

" . . . Mix up more in community affairs. Why not go to some parties and dances? Get yourself a lady friend. . . ."

His deep supplicating eyes stared wildly at his mirrored self, considering this proposal.

Twelve

To say that suspicion had already centered on Buster Crow was a severe understatement. His name entered promptly every discussion and informal caucus held after the death of Carey Miller, and the later murders were oil poured upon flames of gossip.

But he had anticipated all this, and had moved to build an alibi at considerable expense, before there was even occasion for comment. If he could not alibi himself in fact, he could in theory. His chief business had been killing, and for hire, and for a long time. He welcomed subterfuges he employed, anticipating each move with secret humor and delight. He thrived on the arduous physical contest in which he indulged perforce. Trying his own hardihood against the elements of nature brought a singular joy.

The Monday after his midnight encounter in Room Twenty-seven at the Continental, Crow hied himself to Denver as fast as the cars could carry him. There was a long wait at the junction; the train was late also; and it was Tuesday noon before he reached the side-street house where recently he had lain sick and comparatively impoverished.

His big tin-strapped trunk bore the name *A. R. Seton*, and that was the name of the original owner. Crow had become acquainted with Seton in a Southern port before the Army went to Cuba, and before Seton died after a racking struggle with malaria. The Austrian gun with over two hundred rounds of 8 mm. ammunition—unprocurable, so far as Crow knew, in the United States —the rifle and the trunk now belonged to Bus Crow, no matter what collateral heirs might wait in vain and in anonymity for this petty accrual from the Seton estate. For convenience and safety, Bus had used Seton's name when he came to Denver, and in this name the trunk was pledged against his unpaid bill at the boarding house.

The landlady was a fat and fluttery widow, trustworthy, but quite determined to realize something from the unpaid account. If Crow had paid her when he first left Denver, he would have had no money with which to buy a horse. So he was compelled to leave the locked trunk behind. The woman had promised to hold it for two months, and was now delighted to have the trunk redeemed for cold cash, to have the bill paid to the penny, and all within a fortnight.

Bus called a hack to take the trunk to the Imperial Hotel, and there he registered again as Seton. Marching now confident in a newly-pressed suit and shiny boots included in his redeemed wardrobe, Bus found a job-printer not far from the hotel. He ordered one hundred sheets of letterhead stationery, when in fact he needed but one: the printer would not undertake the order for less.

86

The stationery was austerely impressive. It read: "Occidental Smelting and Refining Corporation. 5 West Monroe Street, Chicago, Illinois," and in minor red script was printed, "A. R. Seton. Western Representative." The letter which Crow now contrived and dictated to the public stenographer at his hotel was a model of effective revelation.

"Dear Mr. Crow," the letter said. "Despite public reports to the contrary, we are still so impressed with the possibilities of mineral wealth in the Pearl City region that we wish to retain you to pursue an investigation as previously discussed. Our own private sources indicate that it will be well worth our while and yours also. The enclosed draft will serve as your retainer. Please remember that you are to discuss your activities with no one, and that it is highly important that the strictest secrecy be maintained. We suggest that you try to appear as a mere cowhand, or a man looking for work, in order to conceal the true purpose of your activities. Very truly yours, A. R. Seton."

When he left Denver, Bus Crow took his trunk along; but the train put him and his luggage down at Olney, a small shipping point forty-two miles east of Pearl City. There, after inquiry, Crow was able to rent a horse and a light wagon; he departed into the hills with his trunk and with two large straw suitcases purchased in Denver. In a remote gulley, free from scrutiny, Bus took his belongings from the trunk, re-packed them in the suitcases, and watched fire consume the wooden frame of the trunk until the metal parts were curling, white-hot, unidentifiable. He drove back to Olney and shipped off the suitcases by express to himself in Pearl City.

The Denver excursion had cost him nearly two hundred dollars, including the board bill and an encounter with a red-headed lady of the evening with whom he quarreled before the night was over, and whom he beat savagely before he left her whimpering in her lonely room. He was not perturbed at this financial outlay. More would have to follow; but the prospective income stretched contentedly into the future—an exciting, bullet-pocked highway paved with greenbacks.

Carefully Bus looked over the horse situation in the Olney region, and he bought a tough young cow pony, sturdy enough to carry his weight. It was a black gelding, and soon Crow would acquire two more horses for his string: a bay and a buckskin. But there was the matter of stabling and provender. For two days he rode the slopes of the Shaving Kettle Range, a low chain of hills bordering the valley of Pearl County. He kept away from the big outfits; he made solitary fires where the smoke could not be seen. He ate birds and rabbits, as he had eaten them in the days of his Apache scouting.

His researches led him at last to the solitary hovel of a deaf half-breed who kept one wife and twenty-odd sheep and goats. Frankly Bus Crow stated his business, which was prospecting, and he showed a sack of worthless ore samples gleaned from hillside rocks to prove it. He soon discovered that his host and hostess could neither read nor write, and that knowledge gave him an added sense of security. He left the black horse; he said that later he might bring other horses to be cared for, and the old man grunted his thanks for the silver dollars Bus paid him.

Crow went on foot for a weary seventeen miles until he picked up a ride in a mover's wagon . . . once more he stood in the dismal single street at Olney, once more he waited for a train.

Most men would have hated the hot hours in the saddle, the wearying circuitous journeys over bad terrain, the riding north when his destination lay truly in the southwest, the knowledge that every mile paid out through the heat of the afternoon must be won back even more slowly by chilly excursions before the dawn. For instance, to travel the sixteen miles to Carey Miller's place, Crow compelled himself to ride seventy-five miles, and that trip had been undertaken twice. Always when he rode abroad, he left Center Street in daylight astride the chestnut on which he had first entered the town . . . it was Janet Miller herself who swore to the authorities that she saw a black horse waiting behind the black-hooded stranger. . . .

The letter typed for him in Denver, on false stationery of the Occidental Smelting and Refining Corporation, eventually spread its simple tidings throughout Pearl City by the easiest possible ruse. Bus Crow took an old wallet from among his belongings and placed the letter therein, together with money and two or three business cards of no great import. He carried this wallet constantly in his coat while he was in town. It was the coat of one of his better suits, salvaged from the tin trunk, and that suit had been made for him by a Kansas City tailor in 1896, and still bore the tailor's label and the name and date, sewn against the inside breast pocket.

All he had to do was wait for some excitement to occur in a moment when he had removed the coat and sat in vest and shirt, playing cards at the Glad Hand. Nearly every day something happened to fetch the patrons pell-mell out through the doorway of the Glad Hand . . . a loose steer scampering over street platforms, a fist-fight . . . even in that late day and age there was a certain amount of careless gun-play when the cowhands liquored themselves.

Bus Crow's opportunity came only three days after the murder of Carey Miller, when fresh gossip was rife and suspicion stared behind his back. There was a runaway about four o'clock in the afternoon. The team attached to a delivery wagon was frightened by a track torpedo discharged in the railroad yards. They came careering through the main street, accompanied by outcry. With all alacrity Crow dashed with other afternoon card-players into the street, and left his coat hanging across the back of his chair.

He followed the runaway down a side street to its termination, with the wagon upended against a feed store fence; and then he stood about until the one injured horse was destroyed, and watched the carcass being dragged away. He went to drink at Cox's Bar, and did not return to the Glad Hand for two hours at least.

Meanwhile his coat, the wallet and the contents thereof were eagerly examined and appraised by Sheriff

90

Ballantine, Ole Paulson and others, with a look-out posted at the front door to tell them if Crow was coming. The one hundred and seventeen dollars in the wallet were at least a minor guarantee of financial respectability, and the letter itself spoke volumes. There was the tailor's label in the coat . . . so, after all, it *was* an affectation of poverty, a pretense at job-hunting which marked Bus Crow's initial appearance among them. Ballantine at least was firmly convinced that the secret of Crow's Pearl City maneuverings was now known—though Ole Paulson professed to disbelieve, however much he might believe in fact.

Ole owned some property out in the Milk Creek neighborhood, and now he went there at odd seasons to look for gold along a water-course that bordered his land. One early morning Bus Crow, riding in his usual tiresome wide circle, with blood figuratively dripping from his hands, within twenty-four hours of the fourth murder—Bus Crow descried the stooped figure of a man clambering among rocks of a dry creek-bed. He hid his horse and made a sly approach upon his belly. He lifted the glasses which were a standard though secret part of his equipment, and for a time he watched Ole Paulson toiling in search for the alleged mineral wealth of the Pearl City region.

Crow went back to his horse; he mounted and rode far to the south before he swung back across the plain to Pearl City. The delightful humor of the situation tickled his risibilities; all alone on the hot range, as the sun paled high and hotter, he rocked in his saddle and howled with laughter.

Thirteen

On the Saturday evening following his receipt of the twelve hundred dollars and the note of advice, Bus Crow stepped within the door of the Elk Run schoolhouse.

He felt a shyness engendered not by fear, but by insecurity from a stark personal source. The room before him called to mind certain festivities of his Missouri childhood, when, battered in soul and in body as he always was, he had come cringing amid kerosene lights and the whining of rosined bows.

In his boyhood it was unthinkable that either of his parents would attend a neighborhood social function. Probably they had been asked long before; Bus did not know, but within the time of his memory no one had bothered to include the family in a merrymaking.

The father was a burly sadist—a coward at heart, whose coarse truculence had got him whipped a dozen times in that region. He avoided his mature contemporaries as the plague; he found sturdy pleasure in bringing his own children, as he called it, "to time." His livestock trembled and stamped when he strode near.

Bus Crow's mother had served her term as a thin

whipping-post, until—reason prevailing over the father's orgiastic villainy—she was spared such overt physical torture, because she could not draw water when her shoulders were black and blue, she could not bite the thread of her sewing when her mouth was swollen.

They lived a life apart; the valley where their frame house stood had a peculiar spookiness of its own. Always it seemed that a child was yelling at the Crows' when men went past with their mules. The farmers and hill-dwellers pitied those children remotely, abstractly . . . they still drove on, they passed by on the other side of their choosing.

So the one public hall of the village would be alert with twanging of the jew's-harps, with the pipes of accordions . . . fiddle reels would twist and bray. The sweet-potato pies, the platters of fried pork would be spread upon the tables; but the Crows would never come with baskets of their own. No more would any-one have thought to send a messenger to the new-freed slaves of the South, or for the Pawnees who galloped a few days' journey to the west.

But Buster Crow—the eldest and consequently the most flailed-alive of the children—would creep some-times from his bed in the barn, and find a way through dark, among basswoods and over rocks, driven by a feverish wonder at the strange demonstration waiting on the journey's end: the spectacle of the dance, the notes of laughter he never heard beneath his father's roof-tree.

A generation before, the same disordered pageant

93

that he saw now at the Elk Run school, had bobbed before his eyes: grown men and women comporting themselves like colts . . . the cheers and hubbub of half-wild young Confederate veterans who wore their hair long, whose fingers seemed encased in iron when they tamped the banjo strings . . . no, no, these were people of a later, and in many degrees a milder, breed. But there was something of the same permanent jauntiness about them . . . and once again the goblin figures of children tagged and scampered on the outskirts, their screeching rose amid the jingle of hoe-down tunes.

In that moment, as long before, Bus Crow's envy of those children and the elders was dried through distillation into acrid musk. He did not love them for the fun they had. He had hated them all, long before, when he clung to a splintery windowsill and stared dark-eyed at mirth amid the lights. Now his hatred was the classic coldness of indifference.

Fourteen

When he entered the schoolhouse, Crow was greeted cordially by Gus Bainbridge, one of the men whom he had been directed to kill. Bainbridge was happy to be a member of the human race, and had prospered mildly for years as the proprietor of a tidy farm establishment in Kansas. A great-grandfather at sixty-six, he felt the stirrings of adventurous ambition again. He had come with his wife some forty months earlier to reconnoiter Elk Run Valley, and eventually to settle there.

His fences stung like a loose lash in the eye of any big rancher who glimpsed them, though (like Simon Teal) Gus Bainbridge had never preyed upon the larger herds round about. Ed Nailey and Davis Arden had done so; but Bainbridge was lodged in their fatal category more through his canny persistence in homesteading land than for acquisitive acts against the proprietors of herds on the open range.

As the boss of a bigger outfit he might have sat amid the ranks of the tight-jawed members of the Stockmen's Club. As their enemy he was marked for extinction.

Now he came to welcome the newcomer, though others in the group where Bainbridge had stood looked askance at the black-browed Crow. They had heard the rumors; certainly they mistrusted the advent of a professional gunman in their neighborhood. But to Gus there was only one course open: to offer the hand of hospitality.

"Come in, come in. Make yourself comfortable."

"Thanks."

Crow's suit, a gray flannel stored among the Denver "plunder," had been pressed by Pearl City's journeyman Chinese. He wore a gray shirt also, and a bright blue necktie he had bought that morning.

He came with fresh color on his hands . . . no one in the Elk Run schoolhouse could see that blood or smell the taint of it.

Bus was embarked upon a deliberate enterprise such as he was unaccustomed to pursue. The strain showed in his face.

"Guess you're Buster Crow, ain't you? I've seen you in town. My name's Bainbridge."

Merciless beyond the power of others to discern, Crow leaped inside his skin when Bainbridge spoke the name. He thought coolly, "Well, it won't be long now. If you only knew. . . ." and all the time he was shaking the puffy hand Bainbridge offered.

"Glad to have you with us, Mr. Crow. Just put your hat over there where those benches are shoved together—"

Crow tried to smile as he said it. "Do I have to check my gun?"

Perhaps five or six men in the entire room were wearing guns, and they had only appeared in public thus armed since the shadow of the unknown killer lay across the country.

Bainbridge laughed. "No rule about that; but we never have any trouble at our doings around here—we don't serve any booze—just coffee and sandwiches."

Crow disposed of his hat, and followed Bainbridge through the thin circle of guests who watched the dance. It was early in the evening: some of the shyer men had not yet poked their courage up to the dancing point, though the merriment of women was already affecting them (shrill, tight laughter, the busy gabbling voices of women who led lonely lives, who saw few friends and fewer strangers through their toiling weeks, and stridently welcomed the opportunity for chatter).

Mattie MacLaird skipped arm-in-arm with a lanky Norwegian cowboy in a red-plaid shirt. Crow observed grimly that whatever the gaudiness of this string-bean's attire, he was no great shakes as a dancer; he was stepping all over Mattie's feet.

Up on the platform from which the teacher's desk had been removed, the orchestra struggled in the clutches of "Miss McCleod's Reel." The caller crouched and trembled, snapping his fingers, wagging a scraggly goat beard at the throng. He brayed up against the low ceiling: "All go home . . . all go home . . . promenade all around the hall . . . ladies to the center and gents circle right." The nasal cry went keening on, resinous as the bows of the two old violins alongside.

"Get in there and dance, mister," ordered Bainbridge.

97

Crow's expostulation was lost amid the caller's repetitious wailing. "Ladies to the center and gents circle round. . . ." Awkwardly a chain of men began to revolve, holding hands, throwing their weight against each other's arms, swinging past the mob of women and young girls who waited hopefully in the middle of the circle . . . Mattie was there, taller than most of the others. She looked a little pale, Crow thought; and then he knew that she was pale because she had seen him.

Her reaction had been a mingling of fear and disgust, and finally (he hoped) fascination.

Bainbridge gave Buster Crow a friendly swat, and propelled him toward the circling string of men. "They need more men: some of those womenfolks have been dancing together."

People broke their hold to admit him; now he was circling with the rest. He looked purposefully at Mattie. Again he caught her eyes, and again she turned her face away.

"Choose your partners. Gents all choose. . . . Step right up in your new store shoes. . . ."

They broke loose and rushed upon the squealing women in the center. Partners were pulled from hand to hand, dragged and whirled in the romping charge. The skinny cowboy was striving desperately to reclaim Mattie, and she seemed seeking him. Her arm was extended as Bus Crow cut swiftly past the youth, blocked him off with a shoulder, and clasped Mattie MacLaird in his arms.

She struggled, she sought to avoid him, to break

away; but he only held her tighter, and swung her until he heard her gasp . . . his pulse quickened at the sound. The tempo was changing; fiddles scraped into measures of "The Rye Waltz" with guitar and banjo players scrambling behind, trying to catch up.

"Waltz your lady, waltz her round . . . waltz her fast and go to town."

Crow asked, "What's the matter? Don't you like to dance?"

She kept her face turned away, refusing to meet his eyes. "Not with you."

"Why not? I'm a good dancer."

They moved now with Mattie's back to the orchestra. Above her head Crow could see that the caller was already tiring after his early evening's exertions. He had been calling these complicated figures for an hour or more; probably he would be willing to let folks continue with the waltz for a time. The caller turned to wipe his forehead, and accepted the coffee which a little girl was offering.

There was less stiffness, less resistance in Mattie MacLaird's body: she had realized sensibly that she must accede to Crow's demand and waltz with him, or else create a scene. They danced well together . . . she would not look at him. . . .

The music changed to "Rye Whiskey" after "The Rye Waltz." Still it was a waltz, still the instruments jangled in that rocking beat, still the boots of the players tapped the floor in time.

Mattie barely murmured as she spoke; he had to incline his head to hear her.

99

"What did you bring to amuse yourself with this time—a rat-trap?"

"Maybe I'm sorry about that. Don't be so stand-offish. Can't a gentleman apologize?"

"You're no gentleman."

He laughed rudely. "Why do you keep turning away? Still looking for that Nordsky string-bean you were with?"

That was the first time she let her eyes stay with him. "I'm not with that string-bean, as you call him. I'm supposed to be with Ed Nailey."

At mention of the name his lips pressed together a trifle more tightly than before . . . there was the splintering in his eyes which had shone when he approached the cattlemen's table in the Glad Hand, weeks before, when first he spoke aloud and told them how many men he had killed.

"Ed Nailey, eh? Well, where is he?"

"He hasn't shown up. I'm a little worried. Folks say," she added, "that he got one of those warnings this week."

"Special friend of yours?"

"No," said Mattie honestly, "but there aren't many bachelors around here."

"And none of them can dance as well as I can."

She looked at him steadily as he guided her about the floor. "No, they can't," she was forced to admit. "Where did you learn?"

"Army posts. When I was a kid I used to be a scout in the Apache war."

In spite of all her earlier humiliation and the stored-up resentment which followed, Mattie was honestly impressed by Bus Crow. He felt it, he delighted in his power. He had found in demonstrated fact that he exerted an amazing compulsion which might cause a woman to be influenced emotionally and sexually against her better judgment, against all intelligence.

He let this strength flow from him now, in every act and expression of which he might be capable, although restrained necessarily by the proprieties of this simple occasion. But Mattie felt the exudation. Her eyes were on him again and again, seeking, exploring, beginning to accept, as music changed, as they still danced together, with Ed Nailey and the long-legged cowboy forgotten.

Fifteen

The last dance was called shortly before eleven o'clock. By the time the hands of the thick, treasured watches of the revelers had reached the hour of eleven, fiddles were crying the historic, "Goodbye, Old Paint." Only seven couples were left on the floor, and the most elderly violinist was already snapping his instrument into its scabbed case.

For some time wagons, topless buggies and saddle horses had been trailing away from the schoolhouse. This was Saturday night but still a morning would come with cows to be milked, water to be drawn, stock to be fed, no matter how early the festival had begun.

There had been the thick meat sandwiches, the soggy cookies stuffed with chopped raisins for the sake of celebration . . . doughnuts had vanished; the coffee made at home and lugged splashing in covered tin pails, and warmed again on the wood stove in the corner: this had been consumed. Smallest children were gathered unknowing from their mothers' laps and carried out in the arms of their fathers . . . eyes would open in sleepy surprise when they found themselves bedded at home. The middle-sized children were routed from nests amid

102

the wraps on benches pulled aside; they had staggered
out, led to the vehicles, yawning and fretting.

> ... I'm a-leavin' Cheyenne,
> I'm bound for Montan' ...
> My horses aren't hungry,
> They won't eat your hay ...
> Goodbye, old Paint. ...

Through darkness bred by the distant thunder that
now hovered low in rocky hills, one horse moved slowly
toward the Elk Run school, not away from it. He was a
pinto, saddled and bridled, but with no rider; he shied
off with pointed ears at the approach of teams that
met him on the road. This horse had been reared in
nearby pastures, and though lately he had dwelt in a
sod-covered stable on slopes to the north, the whim of
his heart lay past Elk Run; thus his hoofs trod the
ground in that direction.

Long before, hours before, in the last fuzziness of
violet twilight, had sounded the note of the rifle shot
... there had been fright and whinnying, a disconcer-
tion at the pull which finally came on one stirrup of the
saddle, and at the weight which dragged for a few
rods, accompanying the pinto's frightened pacing, and
then fell loose.

The horse stood awhile in dry mist; he spoke to
another horse that came near; then he was wary of a
man's figure stalking on foot in the dusk, and he galloped away.

The schoolhouse, perhaps ... he had gone there

much of late . . . he should not return to his stable; only
lately had he been saddled at the gate of the makeshift
corral. Notion of the schoolhouse stayed with him, and
the dimmer but stronger recollection of the barn and
pastures he knew beyond the creek before he was sold
away. So his erratic course took him ever to the south
through evening silences, though he munched at grass
along the way. So he came up to the lights and the
movement . . . there was noise across the ranges to
the west: the rumble of a storm that brewed its liquid
in the sky. The pinto horse stood with bowed head and
waited, nor did he know for what he waited, or why.

Among the last dancers inside, Mattie MacLaird
moved in the clasp of Buster Crow, her crisp hair close
against the gray flannel. . . . Gus Bainbridge left the
doorway and started toward the hitch-rail where his
horse and buggy were tied.

Soon there rose a murmur from people saying their
goodbyes on the steps. The talk ran inside like water;
the last dancers—those nearest the door—broke apart
and hurried to join the crowd around the pinto.

Mattie's hand closed sharply on the arm of her partner.

"What's the matter?"

"Those people—they said—Ed Nailey's horse—"

She was running to the door; Bus Crow followed
her.

Outside, their faces dulled in the half-light, though
sharpened now and again by the twitch of electricity
overhead, men examined Ed Nailey's saddle. Bainbridge
rubbed his hand on the sticky leather and then looked

104

at his hand. Someone struck a match . . . several people began to speak at once in low tones.

"We'd better start looking along the road north of here," said Bainbridge. His voice was wire-thin as he struggled to conceal his emotions.

Mattie had not moved off the step. She stood with hands tight against her skirts . . . vaguely she recalled that this was where she had stood often, in brighter and happier moments, to ring the little hand-bell with which she summoned children from their recesses.

She could not speak these thoughts to the big man whom she felt standing close behind her. All she said was, "Another one."

Crow cleared his throat. "I'd better get my horse and help look for him."

"You don't know this Elk Run country well enough," Mattie told him drearily. "There's nothing you can do." She turned in the extremity of surrender, and the words fell rapidly from her mouth. "Will you ride home with me? I'm afraid."

He looked down at her. "But you're not afraid to ride with me?"

She managed a faint smile. "Not unless you've got another mouse-trap handy."

Thunder rumbled closer, as if meditating brutally about what had happened to Mattie at the Glad Hand, and what had happened to Ed Nailey this night—as if suggesting all the deviltries practiced before, and new deviltries to come.

. . . When they rode into the Mason dooryard and

dismounted near the porch, with lightning quickening, they saw a sheet of paper billowing in the breeze, stabbed with a nail against the woodwork.

Mattie stood frozen in this first tense perception. She imagined that old Mr. Mason had received a warning: one of those dire missives such as had been fastened to other houses in the region. Bus Crow was solidified behind her. *After all*, he thought, *I'm the only one who goes around leaving notes like that. Who the hell—?*

Together they crossed the porch, and the paper flapped in lemon-colored glare. A cargo of hollow barrels seemed dumped out, rumbling across the rangeland of Elk Run. Bus Crow felt for his match-box.

Dear Miss MacLaird, Mrs. Masons sister had a stroke over in Kettle Hollow. Not bad but we have drove over there for the night. Hope you dont mind stayin alone.
Respectfly,
B. J. Mason

Crow and Mattie stood in darkness again, except for the increasing explosions of the gathering storm.

He told the woman, "I'll put up your horse before I go."

There was a calm, almost cryptic quality about Mattie's reply. She might or might not have intended an invitation other than the one expressed by the mere words she uttered. Crow could not tell what she meant.

"You'd better put your horse in the stable, too, Bus. There'll be room—as long as they're gone."

He stood regarding her silently.

106

"It's going to rain cats and dogs pretty soon," she said.

"I'm used to riding in the rain."

Again the lightning flared on her face. "I think— A big storm—"

There would be an element of yielding if he gave way to her request, and stayed. They would be alone in this small house, untouched by the march of other people across lonely land on that night. This was the woman who had appealed to him when he met her first, in her black silk, flavored with her perfume . . . it was her body on which he had snapped the wire claw of vengeful idiocy; and yet that was the same body he felt drawn to possess. Somehow she appeared less inviting to him than ever before, standing abandoned and forlorn in her riding clothes, and with the nervous lightning flickering.

Yet he could not bring himself to accept the alternative. *By God,* he thought, *I guess she's got claws, too, and somehow she's sticking them into me.*

He said gruffly, "I'll stay with you."

Still neither one of them knew exactly what Mattie might mean in her invitation—Mattie least of all. Crow held no knowledge of what limit he might reach in his desire on this night, nor of the pattern of the hours ahead.

The storm struck hard before they opened the door. Wind came with it.

Sixteen

Throughout the first sharp fury of the storm they clutched in the common child- ishness of people confronted by an ele- mental display. Mattie held Bus Crow's hand; she laughed and squealed, she closed her eyes in reflex each time the lightning snapped close. They thrilled together in the flare that stung the windows, and their voices rose high to surmount the million drumsticks of rain beating the tin skin above their hands.

Bus Crow had gone plunging away with an old slicker of Mr. Mason's over his shoulder. He led the horses into the stable, found a lantern, got down the bedding, cared for the animals with the skill and ease of a lifetime's experience. When he came back he was greeted as a hero. The fresh hot coffee Mattie had made was better than coffee at the schoolhouse; there was good cold beef, and the baking-powder biscuits of morning had been warmed up for him.

He wondered once, while he was eating and as he caught the woman's gaze across the oilcloth-covered table—he wondered when was the last time he had sat in a house with a woman offering hospitable gifts. He wondered when was the first time . . . there had not been many such occasions. Then with implacable force he swung the doors of memory and of imaginative speculation. He turned the knobs, bolted the doors, and lived once more in the present; he found the present acceptable.

They sat beside a lamp placed on a flimsy table in the sitting room: a lamp with china shade hand-painted by Mrs. Mason, all aglare with colored poppies. . . . They held the stereoscope, they passed the instrument back and forth, they saw the Sphinx and Pyramids, the Coliseum of old Rome, the Arch of Triumph . . . Bus Crow talked a little about Cuba. Mattie had never been east of Missouri or west of Utah. She asked him questions, and he was pleased to award her a few souvenirs from the lore of his traveled sophistication. He even culled out some phrases of Spanish as she listened in awe. He began to talk in Apache, and abruptly hated himself for doing it.

What was he—a young country buck, trying to spark the hired girl, working deliberately to impress her? Crow was ashamed—not because he feared that she would recognize his boasting for what it was—but because he knew that truly he was built of more dangerous stuff. Any two-bit drummer from Kansas City could have made the journey to Cuba on a Government transport—and a great many of them had. Half the worn-out old desert rats of the Southwest could jabber to the Apaches or to Navajo or Pueblo Indians in their own lingo. . . .

Bus Crow's pride should not stem from anything as trivial as this. His might was conceived in a percussion cap, flavored with the nitric smell of burnt powder, shaped by strokes of rifling in a gun-barrel. His majesty was a legend and he knew it. He dared not discuss it with this woman, and would have scorned to do so even if it had been wise.

The throbbing beat of the rain, the sweep of winds whipping it, were idling at last . . . thunder tumbled away into the mysterious northeast, growling like an old dog. The lightning was remote, more feeble, only a loose flicker now and then that did not even mark the windows in contradiction to the lamplight.

But water still came down: an accumulation of moisture draining from odd hollows of the ill-shaped roof, flowing through and over sediment in the eaves-trough, splashing from a spout above the barrel.

The clapboard walls were thin. There were no laths or plaster coating to deaden the sounds—just the frail dressing of light boards inside, with cheap wallpaper to cover them—and thus the flow through the eaves-spout and into the barrel was close in sound, bitter and possessive in Buster Crow's consciousness.

He stirred restlessly . . . the water was always there. It lived in the stereoscopic cards as well. *Famous Wonders of the World,* said the title on the box. *Fifty Views Complete. $1.25* . . . and why did they have to put in Old Faithful? Tourists gathered above the rocks of Yellowstone in their static poses. They were in the garb of at least fifteen years before, they stared at Nature's marvel, they saw steam burst on high . . . Niagara Falls: the torrent swept on and on. . . .

Mattie inserted another card in the slide and passed

the stereoscope over to Crow, but he refused it. "Guess I've seen enough of these."

The woman laughed a little. "Anyway, they served to pass the time."

That angular string of rainwater hanging from the spout a few feet away, dark and cold in its twist, dissolving to a pattern as it strung out into the hollow reservoir, the leaky barrel . . . as a taut chain, descending like the very machinery of the devil . . . it brought Bus Crow out of his chair, it lifted him aloof from the creature comfort he had been sharing.

Thus he stood gazing down at Mattie's pretty, good-tempered face. He regarded the softness, the fleshy female warmth of her countenance, and those other softnesses of which a man could only dream because they were buried politely beneath the fabric of her clothing.

He told himself with angry reiteration that she was a weak thing, shaped only to be twisted and tortured. She had not the strength to combat him if she wished, and therefore she was insipid and worthless.

"Too bad you got stuck with me," he said. "It was your idea. Too bad you didn't have something more interesting around here than a bunch of stereoscope cards!"

On a shelf the clock kept stroking in its wooden case, its mechanism talkative behind a painted sunset on the little door. The clock ignored the shapeless fury within Buster Crow . . . so he hated it and thought of smashing the instrument into fragments.

Mattie's eyes were turned up at him, darker than

blue, mildly pitying . . . and smoky flickers from the dried-out lamp . . . you could smell the wick charring, there was oil needed.

"You're sick," Mattie said softly.

"There's nothing the matter with me."

She rose from her chair and touched his hand. Crow realized for the first time that he had been standing with his hand clamped upon his forehead.

"Bus," said the woman, "there *is* something the matter with you."

He snarled, "It was hot today. I had to do a lot of riding in the dust. I got a little hot—that's all."

But she had taken him by the hand and was leading him behind the rocking-chair. There waited an old sofa, comfortably upholstered, with one end elevated and an antimacassar tacked thereon. Mattie pressed gently against Bus Crow; she was compelling him to sit on the edge of the couch.

"Lie down quietly for a while."

"What do you mean—lie down?"

"I want you to rest."

He lay back gingerly, resting his weight on one elbow, his shoulder adjusted to the raised portion of the couch. Mattie was kneeling before him. She pulled at his boots . . . across the short distance of the room in the now-sodden emptiness of night, that eaves-trough water still made its sound.

Bus Crow had closed his eyes, but he felt her lifting his sock-feet, bringing them up, placing them on the sofa. He heard her go into the kitchen, and then her light steps approached once more. There was wetness:

a limp fold of cool cloth placed across his eyelids. She had soaked her clean handkerchief in water from the drinking-pail, she had brought it to him as a bandage for his hurt.

Now she was sitting on the floor; he could hear her as she adjusted her limbs and her clothing. He thought that he could smell her hair, rising wiry in the fading lamplight near his face.

The meditative plaint of her voice. . . . "It's just as if no one had ever been kind to you before."

"You're right."

"Why weren't they?"

"I wouldn't let them be kind to me." Quickly he wrenched himself around on the sofa and lifted his hand as if to tear the folded handkerchief from his eyes. "Oh, stop that water!" he cried.

There was a long silence reaching into the darkness that wrapped him. "You mean the eaves-spout outside? It'll stop in a minute. The rain's let up."

He lay stiff. He heard only his own breathing and hers, with the cruel piccolo song of rain-water beyond.

"Bus."

"What?"

"Why can't you stand to hear water trickling? You acted that way—you acted funny—out by the horse-trough in back of the Glad Hand."

He began to speak words that he had never uttered before, and yet they had dominated his consciousness waking or sleeping through the years. "Oh," he said, "it happened a long time ago when I was a kid in Missouri."

"Missouri. I came from there, too."

"Well, maybe your childhood was better than mine. Mine was hell on earth. I had a father who beat the tar out of me from the first time I can remember. My mother— We were pretty poor, and she had a lot of trouble. There wasn't much she could do."

He went on, his hard voice had become a flutter. "I had one friend, though—wonderful—the best friend in the world. His name was Brownie," and as he spoke the name, it seemed that in remotest distance a collie was barking happily, almost as if Brownie heard his name invoked and was answering the summons from the grave.

. . . It was a woodsy place among the rocks, Bus Crow said—dim and pleasant. Spring water swelled in a tiny flow, filling up a natural depression among the stones, and stealing away as a rivulet. There were the creek and the shallow ford, and a crude road that came up from the ford to pass over a timbered ridge.

It was along this road that he had run, aged nearly twelve, carrying the old bucket with him. The scars of the hiding he had sustained on the previous night were raised and raw across his back and buttocks. His father had used a tug-strap that time; Bus Crow remembered it well.

But there was always Brownie . . . the dog, his thick coat studded with burrs, his ears raw from ticks—the collie had slept with Bus in dirty blankets above the corncrib built into their barn. The collie escaped the beatings aimed at him, usually. Brownie was quick as

114

a cat on his feet. He knew when to fade through a doorway at the first indication of a club lifted or a missile hurled. He could leap as fast as a deer; Saul Crow might never catch him; he could only growl and threaten. He told Bus to keep that damn dog out of the haymow. He said the dog would spoil the hay; though one might wonder how that could be, since most of the hay was filthy, mouldy and matted, left over from previous seasons.

But it was easy enough, after Saul Crow was safely shut in the house, and the lamp blown out. Bus kept a long plank hidden under the eaves. He could shove it down to the ground, lean it from the upper window of the loft. Brownie would climb with steady confidence, hooking his blunt toenails against the cleats nailed for that purpose, and thus Buster Crow secured his bedfellow, his priest, his love. He could sleep, with the happy dog smell about him once more. . . .

In dreams they excavated a thousand ground-hog dens; they even found wolf cubs among the sycamore roots . . . gay and naked they splashed across the streams. They ate fresh doughnuts together in imagined generous kitchens of the rural gods. Hot cookies stuffed with currants and butternut meats: these treasures Bus would break in pieces for the collie, and make him beg. In dreams they ate as many as they wanted. . . .

So on this morning with every nosegay of elderberry lace pure in the sun (he thought that he could remember each leaf now, each dry stone he turned in the road with his buckskin feet, and he even thought he could remember the clarity of the redbirds)—on this morning he and Brownie were filling the bucket at the spring, in response to orders, when the movers came past.

First there was a rattle-trap wagon, covered, drawn by a nondescript team. It came down the hill into the ford, it rumbled through, and the boy and the dog watched. A man and a woman sat on the seat; the usual junky household equipment was hung all over the wagon.

"They're just movers," Bus told the dog. "Just movers, Brownie. They're going out West," and then two boys came following along on their gray horse.

One of the boys was some years older than Bus; he carried a single-barreled shotgun. The second boy was about Buster's size. He had his arms around his brother, holding on. Bus didn't like them when he saw them. They made him think of other boys there in his own neighborhood, people bigger than he who had ranted against him, laughed at the over-sized pants he wore— who had held him up by feet and hands to offer what they called a "stretching" when he tried to fight them.

There were words of query and challenge passed back and forth as always when individuals met in the open hostility of a suspicious childhood . . . what do you think you're doing with that old bucket? . . . what do you think you're doing with that old dog? . . . well, what do you think you're doing with that old shotgun? . . .

They bragged that they were going out West with their folks. They promised that they would shoot some Indians. The bigger boy swore that for two cents he'd shoot that old dog, and Buster Crow soared from the spring to give the battle he was forced to give.

The smaller boy had slid down from the horse, they were locked together, thudding and snarling in the dust . . . all the time Bus remembered that Brownie was barking in threat and alarm. Somehow or other during the battle the elder boy dismounted also. Bus remembered that he saw him standing with the gun in hand.

Perhaps Brownie tried to attack this enemy; Bus didn't know. He recognized only the roar of the shotgun fired suddenly. He heard the last rapid barking that broke in a squeak and left a silence more hideous than any sound ever made before.

And both boys were now piling on their horse, and fleeing to catch up with the wagon that had gone on ahead. Buster could not hear the hooves of their horse, nor the splash in the ford. He had the heavy dog; he was trying to work over him; he didn't know what to do.

He saw where the charge had gone through the darling fur, and his hands found the hole on the opposite side of the darling body . . . his hands were drenched, fanning about in the warm blood-flow, trying to pull the ruptured hide together, trying to reconstruct the flesh blown loose. He was trying to be Jesus to this. Lazarus; his own prayers and his own shrieking sounded as if they came from the other side of a forty-acre field.

There was the spring, the bucket brimming, the icicle of water striking down eternally, with its serene chatter of the comfort of caves (fabled subterranean palaces of crystal encrustations from which it had emerged), of secret fairy splendors that Bus and Brownie had dreamed about when they were digging for ground-hogs and hoping to enter a limestone citadel, replete with forgotten treasures of vanished road agents —stuffed with the tomahawks and war-bonnets that Indians had left there a hundred years before—

Water beamed and spoke, a river came from the bucket . . . the stream was turned to pink as Bus Crow tried to manage the only therapy he had ever heard of.

"I guess," he told Mattie MacLaird, "I wasn't very smart. I had seen folks faint, I'd seen them knocked cold, and then they threw water in their faces to bring them to. I guess I thought that would work with Brownie; I kept throwing water on him. I don't know how long—maybe it was an hour—I don't know. Of course it wouldn't work. He was dead as a doornail the minute he got shot."

And in his heart the prayer kept uncoiling: a seemingly endless tape with his urgency and his desire printed thereon, although he did not have the words or the detachment to speak this prayer to Mattie. She had to find it somewhere under the shamed mutter he made . . . *you got to come back to life, Brownie. You're the only thing I've got—the only thing I love. The only thing— The only— Oh, dear God, please, please—*

The Creator refused him, so he would hate the Creator forever; he would scorn His name; he would affront Him whenever he could.

He hung the picture in Mattie's mind; she could see it clearly, and shuddered in the seeing . . . the ragged

118

child soaked and bloody by the spring, his hand falling away from the dog's body as he lifted his wet face and let his features freeze into a pattern of unalterable malevolence. She heard the little-boy voice going on and on, speaking the hard truth he had come to know.

So that's the way it is. All right, now I know what to do. I'll kill, too ... I'll always kill. I'll shoot them down. I'll shoot the whole world. I'll get a man and keep killing and killing, and behind him the wealth of the spring would come forth. Its chaste unyielding tone would be reflected in the careless dripping of any tap left unclosed, of any crude faucet where the plumbing was worn ... *I'll get rifles and pistols, I'll kill anybody that gets in my way ... I'll kill anybody I take a notion to.*

The faint wet voice of the eaves-trough was long since stilled. Bus Crow's voice kept coming from the shadow beside Mattie. He had removed the handkerchief from his eyes; he crouched in the low lamplight with his chin on his hands, his elbows on his knees.

"I was just a kid when I ran away. I started killing the first chance I got. Yes, I really liked to kill—I always have. The first one I got was a Mexican kid. He tried to get gay with me. That was after I drove to Texas with some folks ... Apaches, Mexicans ... I rode with the Army as a scout. Then I was a range guard ... special police officer two or three times, deputy sheriff twice ... working for a detective agency, too, and for the railroad—special agent for the railroad. Then I went to the War."

He said, not as if speaking to her, but as if he were addressing the immense jury of those he had already slain (all waiting, voiceless and submerged, beyond those clock-ticked walls)— "I don't say that's the whole reason I'm like I am—Brownie getting shot, and that spring water, and everything. Maybe it was because my father knocked the life out of me all the time, or maybe— Guess sometimes I think it *was* that water, just going on and on as if nothing had happened. Guess I'll hear it always—hear it until the last moment I'm alive—"

The woman's voice was low and rapid; they were alone in the room, alone in the whole storm-wet valley. "Oh, poor darling! Isn't there room for anything but murder in your heart?"

Dry and smoking, the wick of the table lamp offered little material for flame. The fire went up, a skinny tooth of orange, trailing its soot against the chimney, blackening it until it seemed the glass must crack. A smell of smoke and the burnt dry wick was all around them, but neither man nor woman moved.

"I don't know why I told you all this—I never told anybody before. Guess I'll never tell anybody again."

"Bus," she sobbed, "look at me. Can't you see the pity I feel?"

He gazed wonderingly, and then the flame died in the lamp. They were in oil-smoked darkness. His mouth was on hers, in hers, all around hers. There on the couch she yielded up the fervor which she called pity; others might have called it frenzy or delight. Whatever the name, Bus Crow and Mattie were together in shared and repeated violence, they were together for hours.

Seventeen

Sky grew gray above the up-ended substance of mountains . . . grayness thinned and brightened to the soft green of peas; then it was ruddy, promising sun. Before the sun came, distant blotches that were the cattle herds could be seen—ragged pools amid the short grass of distant miles—patient, grazing again, no matter how lashed they had been by rain at night. The air was thin, chilly with the approach of autumn, but there were still a few bold larks left to rise and whistle.

Bus walked out on the porch, tying his necktie as he came. He held his hat crumpled under his arm. He closed but did not latch the door behind him; then, as a breeze leaned against the door, it began to swing open once more. Bus Crow stood gazing at the sunrise.

He was as ashamed as any young virgin who admits in the sanity of light that she has allowed a sin to be made against her. The love passages of the hours had only flavored him in their moment. They had colored but never blasted the rock around his spirit.

To ride away as quickly as possible, to forget the childish, the pitifully delicate attentions he had given and received in a manner never practiced before: this impulse occupied his whole being. It made his fingers flounder as they tried to wrap the blue silk tie into place.

Mattie MacLaird knew too much about him now. He was inclined to hate her for her knowledge of his essential humanity. He could not hate her wholly, but at least he could assume the toughness which ordinarily he wore against the world.

Crow's horse held its head across the top pole of the corral; the animal recognized its master, and spoke of it. Perhaps that sound awakened Mattie, perhaps she felt only the brush of breeze that traveled through the living-room. But she rose from the sofa, she pulled the old patchwork quilt aside, and followed Bus Crow.

The door creaked. He heard her step but still he did not turn. His hands worked at reshaping his hat.

"Bus."

He neither turned nor replied.

"Bus," she asked, "were you going away without kissing me goodbye?"

"I did kiss you."

"But not goodbye."

He turned, he supposed that he was contriving some appalling rigidity of his features. The woman looked at him with a pleading to be resisted certainly if ever he had resisted anything in his life.

"I ought to have gone a long time ago. I'm no good for you."

"I love you, Bus."

He wielded the sharpest hatchet-blade of his antipathy. "I don't want you to love me. By God, can't you understand? You poor little— Listen, sister. I'm a professional killer. I've killed seventy-one people!"

. . . Well, she knows now . . . no, maybe she doesn't. She's a woman (oh, Jesus, what a woman! I can't forget) and so she's a fool. She's going to go on talking about love, claiming me, trying to tell me what to do, bawling around. . . .

His naked soul screamed from the wasteland in which it rode forever. "Mattie, get it through your head: I never talked to anybody before, the way I went on with you last night. Believe me—I'll never do it again. Do me a favor, will you? Forget I was here."

He turned away, despising the horror and hunger in her face. He refused longer to look at her; but he carried the imagined spectacle of how her face might appear—he carried it with him for hours—until at last, summoning the murderous strength of habit, he could batter the illusion to pieces, break its nose and black its eyes, roll it into the ditch of his past.

Soon he would forget that Mattie had ever held appeal for him.

"I'm saddling up," he said. "So long," and he went to get his horse.

Eighteen

In quite another direction from the route taken by Crow, a group of men were gathered by the roadside in that same hour. People on horseback had discovered the thing they saw; others came with buckboards. Foolish women were even holding their children up in order to get a better view over the heads of the crowd.

But almost all they could see were the booted legs sticking up over a little hummock next to the road . . . Ed Nailey had been shot in the back.

Gus Bainbridge was there. He was not only infuriated by the cold-blooded killing of an acquaintance, but also disgusted at the making of a public spectacle out of this tragedy.

He had covered Nailey's face with his own coat, and he kept urging others to keep the women and children back, to order them away.

"There's Wilson Ruder there, alone in his wagon," said Bainbridge. "Let's get Nailey into that and take him to town. Can't leave him laying here in the sun."

Gare Stiver and one or two others suggested that perhaps they had better leave Nailey's body where they had found it, for Sheriff Ab Ballantine to see.

"What's the use?" cried Bainbridge. "That old coot —he's no good. He hasn't smelled out a single clue to any of these murders. I tell you, gentlemen, we've got to take matters into our own hands!"

Stiver swore, and declared, "That suits me. Somebody is fighting us fellows with guns. I claim we ought to fight back the same way."

"Somebody's fighting us with money," said Bainbridge meaningfully. "We'd better fight back with the same weapon." He looked closely at the faces around him, and saw no dissent.

Sunday evening, thought Bainbridge, might not be an appropriate time to hold a meeting. But surely by Monday night the majority of the small ranchers—recent settlers in the county, including all those who were proving-up claims by benefit of the laws of their land— these people could all be notified. By Monday evening they would have time to reach Pearl City, the best intermediate point.

Accordingly on Tuesday it was published abroad that the Pearl County Ranchers' Association had been formed, and was prepared to offer five hundred dollars reward for information leading to the arrest and conviction of the murderer or murderers of any of the following: Carey Miller, Charles Bevin, Simon Teal, Edward Nailey. Within a week, State authorities had doubled the reward.

This news was found interesting by a man named S. F. Rochelle, when he sat in his office more than two hundred miles away, examining an item in the paper.

". . . A tidy little sum of one thousand dollars,"

purred the newspaper account, "which ought to tempt some bold detective to the utmost."

Speedy Rochelle (christened Stephen at birth) did not consider himself especially bold, but he did have a hearty familiarity with danger. Less than a year and a half before he had been given up for dead; he had lain unconscious and nearly neglected for a day and a night, until the very stubbornness of his pulse and respiration caused the surgeons to look further into the matter.

With consciousness and strength he found amusement when the story was related to him. He was a man who could laugh at himself; he had an easy-going self-confidence.

Born in Louisiana during the War, carried to Texas at an early age, he had developed a quiet passion for the cattle lands of the West, though later he was taken by an uncle to Washington and educated there. While very young Rochelle was made a deputy sheriff in his adopted nation of Texas; when the sheriff of the county was thrown by his horse and relegated to invalidism, he resigned and Rochelle became sheriff.

Promptly he ironed out a range war which had been by turns bloody and legalistic—and forever provocative and expensive—for more than ten years. Whatever plaudits young Rochelle earned, he did not enjoy the necessary delving into politics entailed by his job; when his term ended he did not seek re-election. He was appointed a deputy U.S. Marshal, and served with contentment in that capacity at various stations throughout the West until the Rough Riders were organized.

Back from the tropics, a full-fledged U.S. Marshal at last and wholly recovered from his wound, Speedy Rochelle had been sitting for some months in an office with his neat shoes on the desk. Throughout this period with folded paper and with scissors he had made a marvelous array of darts, accordions, bunnies whose ears would waggle, and little paper soldiers holding one another's hands in a long and identical row.

. . . The item about the Pearl City murders struck deep within the soft cloak of Rochelle's somnolence. (He took fabulous pride in the laziness of his body, the measured ease of his deep-throated voice, and above all in the fact that he kept his hair cut short so'that he should not have to bother parting it.)

On the morning when he read this latest item about the Pearl County assassinations, he tossed the paper aside and leaned back impassively in his swivel chair. For a time he played with an historic bullet attached to his watch-chain. Then, as if arrived at an important decision, Rochelle lifted his foot and shoved against the desk, pushing himself backward in the chair. The little casters grated and squeaked . . . Thus he voyaged toward the telephone fastened at a fairly low point on the wall. Rochelle had had to have that phone moved when he took over the job there: he was a foot shorter than his predecessor.

Reaching the wall, he glanced wearily up at the telephone. It was unseasonably hot . . . this was all too much of an effort. Eternally Rochelle acted the role of sluggard, even when no audience stood handy. He solved his momentary dilemma by reaching up and pulling down the long movable arm on which the transmitter was fixed. Still without rising he spun the crank and lifted the receiver. It took time, but soon he was talking with his superior in Denver.

"Colonel? This is Speedy Rochelle ... I said Speedy ... Thank you kindly, and how are you? ... I'm going to take a little trip. . . . Yes, Colonel, he's coming to take charge of the office tomorrow. . . . Vacation? I asked you, Colonel, what would I do with a vacation— just lie around? . . . Oh, I guess maybe Pearl City ... You can't tell: I might find some pearls ... Thank you, sir. Goodbye. Yes, I did say pearls."

Rochelle hung up the receiver, and at last rose from his chair. When he spoke he was speaking only to himself, but in a firm and audible voice.

"Or maybe swine."

He checked in at the Continental House in Pearl City late the next afternoon. From the first he made no secret of his presence or of his identity. He was even gratified two days later to observe the following item in the Pearl City *Weekly Ledger*. This was fruit born of a professional visit to the editor.

> An echo to the recent cold-blooded killings which have horrified this region is found in the arrival of Marshal S. F. Rochelle, who is here to confer with local authorities. Marshal Rochelle is stopping at the Continental House while in our fair city, and asks that any persons having information which they think might bear upon the assassinations to please get in touch with him there.

Drawling calmly, seeming half-asleep at all times (but meticulously polite to even the broken-down old ex-miner who did the chores of bell-boy and valet at the Continental) Rochelle made himself a prominent figure in the town before the end of the week. That he might court danger in so doing did not even seem to occur to him. That he would unavoidably be deluged with pointless clues, with the reiterated suspicions of quarreling neighbors, and even with the necromantic fantasies of a local deaconess who affirmed that she had seen each of the killings take place in a dream— these truths did most certainly suggest themselves to Speedy Rochelle. But he felt that, somewhere beneath the tangled underbrush of conjecture and fancy, he would perceive little green shrubs of fact.

Ballantine he quickly recognized for the disordered old politician he was; but at least Ballantine had in his possession the four shell-casings distributed by the murderer after the crimes, and he was perfectly willing to hand those over to such a dignitary as a United States Marshal.

The shell-casings conveyed certain information to the sleepy-visaged officer. He could not quite make out the letters or numerals, or decipher their import. He would have to send his evidence East in order to do that.

But Rochelle knew burnt smokeless powder when he saw and smelled it . . . 8 millimeter or .315 caliber. He thought of a Lebel rifle first, but soon recalled that in the Lebel the cartridges were held in a tubular magazine—spring-fed, if he remembered correctly . . . there was the 1895 Mannlicher: that had a box magazine. A number of those guns had been captured in Cuba; and Rochelle, forever fascinated by small arms, had examined one.

The marks on these empty shells seemed to suggest a box magazine. He thought it as simple as that: he would only have to find who in all that region owned an 1895 Mannlicher.

Within the hour after he reached Pearl City the name of Bus Crow had been reiterated in Speedy Rochelle's ears a dozen times. He was not disposed to take his would-be informants very seriously. Certainly he had heard of Crow long before this . . . it was in the back of his brain that he had met the man somewhere or other. Rochelle felt inclined to disregard the importance of Crow in the case, simply because he was such an obvious suspect.

On Thursday, however, with Sheriff Ballantine's whispered affirmation of Crow's complete innocence sinking into his brain, and with the reasons for that belief extolled, Rochelle was moved to send a telegram. He sent it in a code which he seldom resorted to, because code seemed such an affectation.

He could not hope to receive an adequate reply to his request until Saturday; but when the wire was delivered to him by the station agent who passed the hotel on his way home to supper Saturday night—when the flimsy pencil-scrawled slip was placed in his hands and had been by him laboriously decoded, Rochelle knew to what port he would steer his course that evening.

People said that Bus Crow hung around the Glad Hand on practically any night, but almost certainly on Saturdays. He had missed only one Saturday night since he came to Pearl City. Bus Crow did, of course, live at the same hotel, but Speedy Rochelle did not wish first to encounter Crow within tight limits; he wanted to meet him in public. He believed that the man was a confirmed exhibitionist and could be observed more properly in his natural state at the Glad Hand.

Now Speedy Rochelle felt chagrined because he had not concentrated on Bus Crow from the start. His Chicago telegram told him the reason for that: there was no such firm in existence as the Occidental Smelting and Refining Corporation—which, according to Ballantine, had engaged Crow secretly to assay the mineral wealth of Pearl County.

Rochelle waited until about nine-thirty before he sauntered into the bar. The crowd was just beginning to warm up; it was a slow procedure, now that Mattie MacLaird no longer sang. Art Schaub did his best at the piano; he even chanted some of the popular songs he played; but his girlish voice could not lift far above the steady grumble of conversation.

Readily enough the marshal spotted Crow. He had received a careful description of the man from the sheriff, he was familiar with his pictures, and he still held the probing notion that at some time, in some town, he had seen this man face to face, and more than once. Where or how, he was not at the moment prepared to say.

Rochelle ordered beer, and began to play with his watch-chain bullet. This object was a favorite possession of his, and he employed it in his favorite mannerism: the same gesture he had been pursuing when he read of the doubling of the reward offered for the Pearl County murderer. . . . It was a lead bullet, conoidal, with a smashed point. In concentration he was always swinging the bullet in a tiny circle. Forever he watched the process seriously as he did this; but seldom did his ears miss a word of any conversation close at hand.

Now and again Rochelle's pale green eyes traveled along the bar or passed over the faces of people at the nearest tables. He saw the tight-drawn, pock-marked visage of Bob Crashaw. He wondered who this man might be, and with blessed ignorance of the future (the blanket and safety of all men) he did not dream that Crashaw would come seeking to kill him.

Bus Crow wore another costume that had been stored in his trunk. It was a brown serge suit, too dark for his natural coloring; it made his face seem blacker, grimmer, fleshier than it really was.

He stood in noisy pride, though his clothing was loose—the coat hung in too-generous folds from his shoulders. Fever had dried some of the meat from Buster Crow's bones. The arduous activity of recent weeks, mysterious and lonely hours spent in forcing himself and his horses across evil terrain, had slimmed him even while he was toughened.

Already he was quite drunk and in a show-off mood. Several loungers, flattered thus at being seen in the company of a notorious man, stood close. They prompted Bus with ready questions as he went on with his anecdote.

Speedy Rochelle sharpened his ears as he edged closer and was able to hear the words.

". . . So I said, 'General, the troops need to have those mules ashore.' And he said, 'But we'll never be able to land those pack-trains at the wharf.' And I said, 'General, just shove the mules overboard and let them *swim* ashore.' Well, that's how we landed our pack-trains in Cuba."

. . . Pretty good, Bus, they were saying . . . that was quick thinking. What did the General say then . . . ?

To Speedy Rochelle there was something so offensive about Crow and about his manner of relating this preposterous anecdote, that he put down his beer and moved close to the group. The big dark man was not able to speak again in response to prompting before Rochelle's good-natured voice had drawled its question.

"Excuse me. Was that on the beach, when the army landed at Daiquiri?"

Bus Crow put down his glass abruptly, and turned to face the marshal, as did the men with him. He looked at the stubby officer with no attempt to conceal his scorn. "What do you know about Daiquiri Beach?"

Speedy Rochelle smiled placatingly, and then his eyes went back to the little core of lead whirling beneath his fingers. "Oh, not too much, mister. I don't know too much about Daiquiri Beach. But you look kind of familiar to me," and all the time he was seeing palms, seeing the ragged scrub and royal palms bending

133

above it . . . smelling manure and feeling the sand-flies sting him . . . he remembered confusion, the attempt of that sprawling circus to pull itself together and form a military operation when too many cooks were spoiling the broth . . . he remembered well. He heard pale green frogs talking at dust in the palmetto fronds. . . .

He heard also Bus Crow's cold question coming down the bar to strike him; he realized that fifty men were listening now where five had listened before.

"What's your name?"

"They call me Speedy Rochelle."

The quick spark of a destruction reviewed or contemplated was in Crow's suffering eyes again. "So you're the marshal. You're the man who's going to solve all these mysterious killings around here."

"I just aim to try." Rochelle's Texas boyhood spoke more readily for him than did his college years.

Men moved aside. Crow towered over the short-legged marshal.

"What do you know about Daiquiri Beach?"

"Let's see. That was just before the battle of San Juan Hill. . . . I always understood it was Colonel Roosevelt who gave the order to swim those mules ashore."

"That's a lie! It was my idea."

It was easy for Speedy Rochelle to ignore any insult or implied threat. He said clearly, "I recognize you. You were one of the mule packers."

All around them men fired glances back and forth . . . here was this stranger, offering successive challenges, marshal or no marshal. . . .

134

"So I was a packer? Well, what was your job?"
Crow had been presented with an uncomfortable truth
—a deflating truth offered calmly and stoically. He
did not like it.

"I was a staff officer. Lazy man's job—just suited
me."

"What was your rank?"

"Major."

As if drawn beyond his power to control, Bus Crow's
gaze was hauled down to the bullet that still hummed
in its twirling. The lead was dull, it could not seem to
catch the light; but the watch-chain gleamed like rarest
jewelry.

"Why the—" Crow's voice seemed to break slightly.
"Why the devil do you keep whirling that bullet?"

Rochelle smiled generously up at the killer as if he
would ameliorate all sin, all hurt committed or even
suggested. "Mr. Crow, that's my own special private
bullet. They took it out of my chest, just after San Juan
Hill. You see," he said, "I was shot in the front. Not
in the back."

If other conversation existed within the range of
their ears and their voices, it was mumbled secretly
behind hands, guarded in shivery whispers. No voices
resounded openly near that bar; only Art Schaub, smirk-
ing, pulsating his shoulders, strove distantly to make
theatrical gaiety of the piano strings.

"Well," came the marshal's valedictory, "it's past my
bedtime. Goodnight, gentlemen. Goodnight, Mr.
Crow." He sauntered from the bar, moving dreamily
toward the door. Crashaw was standing so close to the

135

marshal that he felt the slow brush of his body as the man went past, away to the front entrance and out.

Almost disbelieving, Bob Crashaw turned to watch Crow. Crashaw was not intelligent enough—he had neither intellectual experience nor observant imagination enough to identify the expression with which Crow gazed after Speedy Rochelle. With more discernment, with a better understanding of heart and ideal, Crashaw might have recognized a prophetic fear in Buster Crow's face.

Nineteen

It did not take six members of the Stockmen's Club long to arrive at a decision
concerning Marshal S. F. Rochelle. They
had not felt themselves in serious jeopardy before;
they did now. They held private conversations. Driscoll
and Springstun visited Jaff Montgomery at his ranch.
Webb called on Britton at his Pearl City house. Peter
Alesworth managed to see everyone, and all the time
he was conducting private investigations also, as fast
as the mails could manage.

When they met in sacrosanct stud-poker session at
the club on the following Wednesday night, poker was
only a mechanical adjunct to their conversation.

"He's a good man."

"I'll take the same."

"Three here."

"I've checked with Denver, Cheyenne, Omaha—even
down in Texas where he came from. He's one of the
best marshals in the business."

"Well, boys, we'll have to take steps. . . ."

Driscoll and Springstun drew cards, but both were
nodding agreement as they drew them, although John

Britton shook his head in severe negation at the same time.

"How many people," Britton wanted to know, "have moved off the range?"

Alesworth told him, "I checked today. Five families."

"That's not enough." Jaff Montgomery voiced the opinion of all when he said it.

Britton asked hopefully, "Think money would talk?"

"Not to *this* marshal."

Britton said apologetically, "I was holding a kicker." He threw his hand down. "Gentlemen—" His voice was sharp with desperation—"haven't we had enough killing already?"

. . . Only the chips talked. Then Alesworth muttered, "Three jacks," and displayed them, and hauled in the pot. "John," he told Britton, "we can't stop now. Let Buster Crow take care of a few more, and they'll all pack up and move."

Montgomery whispered, "Let Crow take care of the marshal before the marshal gets him."

Alesworth said nervously, "No, no! That would be too obvious. It might give away the whole show—might even backfire on us. No, whichever one of us did the actual hiring of Crow—he must have approached him through another man. Now, let him hire that other man to—shall we say *approach*—the marshal?"

Old Springstun grunted, "The quicker the better."

Britton began, "Gentlemen, there's already been too much—"

"We'll take a vote," Alesworth interrupted. "Majori-

138

ty wins. If we vote to do it, we'll fold this game and leave the club separately right now. We'll all go home —supposedly. The man who's going to do the job can get busy. And let me say this: tonight wouldn't be too early."

"One of these days," came Britton's defensive wail, "our chickens are going to come home to roost."

"The hell with our chickens!" Jaff Montgomery cried. "Look here: we've all got cards. Everybody in favor of this, turn up a black card; those not in favor, turn up red."

Their hands spread and shuffled, spread again the few cards before them. Their knotted fingers bent the corners of the cards . . . they saw the suits . . . diamonds, clubs. . . .

Alesworth asked, "Everybody ready?"

There was no reply.

"Then let's consider the motion carried," and Alesworth flipped over the ace of spades.

Montgomery's lips were pressed together, turned in between his teeth. He sighed, and then revealed the card he had selected: six of spades.

Driscoll turned the king of clubs; Springstun, deuce of clubs; Webb, ten of spades.

They were all looking at John Britton. His face showed his defeat, even as silently he beseeched a reconsideration. Then he made a quick gesture, turning a card and slapping it violently with his palm as he did so. He had turned the queen of hearts. That was not much of a surprise to anyone.

Montgomery said quietly, "You're out-voted John."

139

Twenty

At exactly forty-seven minutes past midnight, S. F. Rochelle was comfortably ensconced on his bed in Room Twenty-five on the second floor of the Continental. He had pillows piled up, and was leaning against them, fully dressed except for coat and boots.

Close beside him a lamp burned brightly and an alarm clock chattered the seconds away. In distant spaces across roofs and through walls, far in the Glad Hand, Art Schaub murdered "General Grant's Grand March."

Rochelle had a wide notebook propped on his knees; he was writing in the book. Again and again he had compiled these notes, considered them, torn them to flakes and poured them into the toilet basin. He had flushed away the data of assembled evidence, which might be evidence in truth and yet which still left his search unresolved . . . 8 mm. cartridges left beside the bodies of all four: Miller, Bevin, Teal, Nailey . . . man in a black hood observed by Mrs. Miller, but never seen lurking any place else . . . Mrs. Miller affirmed she saw a black horse . . . Bus Crow never seen riding any horse except his chestnut . . . contents of a letter in Crow's wallet as testified by Ballantine and Paulson. . . .

Rochelle told himself a hundred times that he was getting nowhere; yet the stub of his active pencil was forever reiterating these facts (and drawing a wonderful variety of four-petaled flowers and transparent cubes among the lines he jotted down).

A .44 Smith & Wesson in a Miles City holster dangled from the bedpost at his right hand. There it could be seen by Bob Crashaw as he stole across the outside roof and planted himself against the clapboards near Speedy Rochelle's unscreened window.

The doors of the Glad Hand stood open for a time. Uncertain chords of Art Schaub's rendition rose louder through the night, and then were muted as the doors closed. Faint and scattered lights peeked from other buildings beyond, but they were not enough to reveal Crashaw plainly. He felt safe, covered solidly in darkness.

Rochelle was chewing his pencil as two whispered syllables came to him. "Marshal."

Speedy Rochelle stared at the window.

"Don't go for your gun. Stick up your hands. I want to talk to you."

The pencil dropped from the marshal's right hand as he lifted his arm. He could not see the man calling to him from the roof: only an open oblong of darkness faced him, empty, but now grown dangerously talkative.

"I said your *hands*—not just one hand."

Surely enough, Rochelle was holding his right hand high, but his left arm lay close to his body.

"Sorry. I can't put up my left hand."

"Last chance. Put it up."

"I'd like to oblige you, mister," Rochelle explained elaborately, "but the Spaniards took care of that. I got shot up pretty badly, and sometimes the muscles won't work. Every now and then I can't move my left arm at all. It hurts, too."

Through this lying utterance, the powerful fingers of his left hand worked, folding the covers back, crumpling the spread, stuffing fabric on fabric in order to crawl among the folds. Rochelle's knees and body concealed his hand. To the man outside he did not appear to move a muscle, and yet already the butt of a snub-nosed .38 revolver was crawling like a black lizard . . . a fraction of an inch at a time, the weapon slid within Rochelle's grasp.

Crashaw (only a disembodied and tuneless voice to the marshal) seemed considering the explanation. "All right. I did hear you got wounded—that's the only reason I'm not shooting now. Just don't try to go for that gun on the bed-post."

Rochelle inquired, "Well, who are you, anyway? Why don't you come in? Maybe we can talk this over."

"They sent me here to get you."

"Who sent you?"

"I don't know. The man in the dark again. He had a gun against my back. Gave me a hundred dollars—said he'd give me another hundred, soon as I'd done the job."

Speedy Rochelle owned the little .38 now; his finger was inside the trigger-guard. "Only two hundred for killing me?" he asked mildly. "I don't come very high."

"That's not what I'm talking about. But I know something: I talked to another man before this—same kind of arrangement. I don't know who paid me."

Clacking noisily, the alarm clock seemed jarring the very platform of the flimsy table . . . Rochelle's elbow was lifting, he was taking aim with his elbow. The lamp or the table itself—it didn't matter which. . . .

"So you talked to another man before. What's that got to do with me?"

The gist of the story came from Crashaw. "There's a thousand-dollar reward for the man who's been doing all these killings. If I told you the name of the man I talked to a while back, and he turned out to be the killer, would you guarantee to split the reward with me? Five hundred dollars—that's more than I'd get for rubbing you out."

By this time he was speaking so rapidly that he uttered only the syllables of an involved and complicated word. "Come on come on speak up is it a deal—!"

"How could I trust you?" Rochelle inquired reprovingly. "That other man couldn't." His elbow flashed against the bedside table.

The blow made agony in his funny-bone; but the table had gone over, lamp and all. Rochelle rolled to the floor after it as the flash of a revolver tore through the open window. The marshal fired simultaneously, but he was rolling so rapidly that the shot went wild.

Nevertheless as he crawled from the floor he recognized contentedly that his timely upsetting of the lamp had saved his life. He ducked back and forth as he went toward the window, he fired again as he ran.

It was this second lucky shot that struck Crashaw

between the shoulders. He had retreated rapidly toward the stairway beyond; he was squarely in front of the window when the .38 bullet found him.

Crashaw staggered on, dying stubbornly. He fired twice more toward the window; but he could not travel with rapidity, and the roof of the one-story building seemed far below him now. He was balancing on an imaginary tight-wire . . . his feet could not find anchorage. . . .

The room behind was brilliant with flames from the smashed lamp. Fire scuttled crackling over the pool of oil. Regardless of the fact that the structure was really paper-thin, and bullets from a heavy-caliber gun could puncture it like paper, Rochelle had drawn back against the wall, close inside the window. He sought to take deliberate aim.

The red blaze worked to his disadvantage, and Crashaw had reached the head of the wooden stairway before the marshal could find him with his sights. The first joint of Rochelle's finger squeezed again; the little gun jumped; with satisfaction the marshal saw that vague figure lurch against the railing where it stood. He watched . . . the figure leaned over farther and farther. The man was extending his hands, and Rochelle thought in wonderment, *Does he think he's diving into water?* Then the rotten rail splintered apart, the figure disappeared. When the dull thud reached the marshal's ears, it sounded like someone dropping a sack of corn off a wagon.

"Well," he thought, "the pitcher's full." He hurried to the commode, lifted a china pitcher and hurled the whole weight of its water against the flames. They were spattered and spread by it, but not extinguished. The slop jar; he thought of that:—it was nearly full— they emptied in only in the mornings. . . . Dirty water did the trick. The room was dark, thick with fumes, and outside in the hallway Rochelle could hear people calling back and forth, unable as yet to detect the core of this excitement—the focal point of gunfire and oily blaze—

Rochelle slid out across the window-sill to that room where the man who sought to murder him had walked. Down the block at the Glad Hand, rear doors were open; people swept out across the livery stable area behind. "Where is it? . . . Who's doing all the shooting? . . . Fetch a lantern here!" Rochelle went pad-padding across the roof toward the broken-railed stairway. He tested the steps cautiously . . . they were sound enough. He descended, and struck a match to examine the death he had made.

". . . It's all right, folks," he told the crowd from the Glad Hand, and others who had come prancing from the rear of the hotel. "Just had to shoot a burglar."

They were all around him. It was Sheriff Ab Ballantine who held aloft the lantern someone brought.

A man said, "It's Bob Crashaw—you know—works for Jaff Montgomery on his cattle ranch!" and Rochelle saw the face of Bus Crow cemented in the glare high above the others.

Crow kept his voice low, and Rochelle recognized that he was sober on this night, however drunk he had been when the marshal saw him before.

"What happened, Marshal?"

"He was aiming to rob me."

"Of what?"

"Of my life, for one thing," and the night was alive with sharper questions, unvoiced in speech but wholly recognizable.

Again Sheriff Ballantine held the lantern close. A tide stole out across the gravel . . . dark moisture that ran from Crashaw's mutilated mouth.

"Yes," said Ballantine, "he's dead, all right. Funny he should try burglarizing—he had a job and all."

Belatedly he was struck by the same thought that ran slyly from man to man throughout the group. "Well now, you can't tell. This might mean an end to all the killings around here—"

"I don't think so," said Speedy Rochelle drowsily.

Twenty-One

Dick knew the way home. Dick was seventeen years old and very gray. He was short-barreled, he showed his Morgan blood in many ways. Although not senile, he had settled into a cozy and extended dotage. Whether his driver was awake or sleeping, Dick knew the way home, and undeniably Gus Bainbridge was sleeping now.

The gray-white horse proceeded at a walk. The low buggy, without any top, had its single seat placed forward above the good-sized box in which provisions could be transported in quantity. Gus Bainbridge was slid well down in the seat, his head turned to one side, his wide-brimmed hat pressed low over his eyes.

Through the line of spindly cottonwoods, a feeble windbreak planted along the lane, Martha Bainbridge looked up from her work as she sat on the porch. In her mind's eye she saw those cottonwoods building themselves thicker of trunk, more generous of leaf; she imagined this afternoon's sunlight shining pleasantly, repeated in the future on every heavy corrugation of the trees' bark, and on the paleness of their upper limbs.

. . . A rustle of the imagined bower, the fairy tufts

of white silk blowing in warm wind when tiny bolls had ripened and split: she saw it all in this moment. And she and Gus would be settled in this rangeland haven until they were very old indeed, and all their folks came to visit. They would sing around the organ on Sunday evenings. Falsetto voices of descendants yet unborn would join the tuneful mustiness of their own tones in, "Let the Hurricane Roar," and other songs related in that family, time out of mind.

All this she prophesied in one contented glance amid slim shadows of the adolescent cottonwoods; then she pressed the dishpan deeper between her knees and went on peeling potatoes. Martha Bainbridge smiled, reassured by the approach of the man to whom she had been married for forty-eight years.

Old Dick came on at a walk—reins arching free from his bridle, sagging from the dry dashboard—loose-held indeed by a driver whose hat still shaded his face.

Not until the buggy had halted near the porch did the world, the beauty and life of Martha Bainbridge dissolve and perish ... there was that continued squeaking of the high front wheel on its dry hub (she had been commanding Gus to grease that wheel for two weeks at least)—the creak of it lowering in pitch until the last revolution halted, and the old horse stopped with a little lurch.

Gus Bainbridge's body altered its position in response to this slight shock of the buggy's stopping. Not until he had toppled over sidewise on the seat could his wife know the reason for his going. She saw the small round hole in the sagging upholstery where his broad back had pressed.

She spoke no word as she arose. There sounded only the dishpan of water falling, splashing, and potatoes rolling heavily and severally across the hollow boards of the porch floor.

. . . So Mattie MacLaird was nearly an hour late in arriving at school next morning. The Bainbridges were the nearest neighbors of Mr. and Mrs. Mason, and like the Masons they had offered Mattie a home when first she came to teach. She would really have preferred living at the Bainbridges'; but the old Masons needed the pittance they asked for board and room—they had no productive little farm behind them in Kansas.

On her solitary ride to the hillock where the school-house stood, the girl tried to pursue a cogent course of reasoning. But her emotions were too torn to allow her this luxury. Hoofs of the little spotted mare kept speaking lightly as they touched the ground . . . when she rode through the gap of hills nearest the school, echoes stung back from the rocks in a flogging chorus . . . *seventy-one* . . . *seventy-one* . . . *seventy-two* . . . *seventy-two*. . . .

She held no concrete evidence in her hands. There was only the assertion, the boast to be remembered, and her earlier revulsion against Crow's attitude of congenital cruelty.

There was the whispered midnight revelation of a boyhood anguish . . . *I'm a professional killer*, he had said with the wickedest kind of pride.

149

But who had ever seen him brandishing the strange foreign weapon that left its metallic spoor throughout the county? Who had ever seen him mounted on a black horse—or on the solitary buckskin which some men had detected galloping amid remote shadows before morning?

Mattie came up to the schoolhouse; she saw a cluster of little people peering from the door long before she got there. They fled at her approach—there was the sound of their scurrying, even a giggle or two—though on other occasions they would have shrieked with glee over Teacher's tardiness.

She came, forcing her face into a smile, trying to expel from memory the dry voice of lamentation she had so recently heard. She stood behind her desk.

Drearily she saw that though the little folks whispered to one another in subdued voices, they seemed unwontedly grave.

"Children, Teacher is sorry she was late. I've been at the Bainbridge place—I guess you all know why."

She put down the examination papers brought from home. "Now, first we'll have roll-call, and then we'll sing—" She tried to laugh. "Are we all here?"

. . . The children in their places, the large eyes, the small chins, the faded overalls and cotton shirts . . . yes, Mary Sours was appearing in all the glory of her new plaid gingham; she had chanted the delights of this gown through the ardure of its manufacture, she was being allowed to wear it today because it was her birthday.

150

Frail things, each in a proper place. . . .

The gap—the noticeable gap on one of the benches between two girls. A vacant chair, so to speak.

"Why—" Mattie's voice soared, trailing into space. She brought it back again. "Where's little June? Where's June Arden? She's never been absent before."

A tall child next to the vacant place arose. She dropped an awkward curtsy. "Please, ma'am, her daddy got shot and killed this morning. They—they found him—just before breakfast—"

Motionless walls, clean-swept floor, bare cracked ceiling: they took the thin words and held them awhile, and seemed reluctant to fling them back to be heard a second time. The girl kept standing there, her eyes winking rapidly, her lip quivering—

Now there was no choice . . . Mattie had rested in Bus Crow's arms, she had felt his weight and heard him telling infant horrors . . . she could remember still amid the pepper of these miseries, the touch, the chuckle, the power of his physical strength which miraculously he had held in subjugation (though it seemed beneath the surface of hair and skin and flesh as compelling, as attractively vicious as a crawling panther).

Yet he had done her no harm, and he had given a fulfillment she had never known before— and a later peace spiritually pathetic, as in the beauty of passionate music remembered.

She heard herself saying quietly, "Children, we will dismiss school for the day," and her statement was lost in the buzz of whispering that rose to claim it.

. . . They bounded away on their ponies. Those who lived near by hiked dancing along the roadways on foot. Mattie MacLaird rode directly to Pearl City. Three of the children were with her for a time, then they turned off, and she was alone in her riding.

Twenty-Two

The old clerk at the Continental House sorted mail. A dozen men read newspapers or chatted together in the long room where Mattie stood motionless before the desk, her eyes upon the ledger that served as a register. It was turned away from her: the names were upside down. But she could not have read them had they been turned properly—blotted as the signatures were, wavering before her eyes.

"The U.S. Marshal is staying here, isn't he?"

"Mr. Rochelle, you mean? Yes, lady. He's here."

"Could you tell him I want to see him?"

"Yes, lady. I'll see if he's in his room."

He turned toward a gate in the fence that made an office of the space behind the desk. The clerk passed on into the hall; Mattie followed hesitantly for a few steps, to halt outside the wide doorway that led from lobby to hall. She heard the warped carpet-slippers of the clerk shuffle up the stairway . . . once again she was mutilating her glove as she had done in an earlier week when she waited in Peter Alesworth's office.

Far in the northeast corner of the room behind her,

one man was seated alone, a newspaper before his face. He had been reading with the split attention of the hunted and the hunter alike. In studied experience he had observed the little headlines before him; at the same time he was conscious of each movement made by men beside the smoking tables or among the groups of low-backed chairs.

He had observed Mattie entering; his face had gone behind the paper again . . . all that she could see of Bus Crow were his boots, his trousers, the top of his hat. He was wearing the pants of his dark-blue suit, and she had never seen him in that. He had a new hat of tan felt, bought only a couple of days before. In these scraps of attire visible to her, there was nothing to awaken a response in Mattie.

Her eyes were glazed, trying to brush aside the veils of fear and confusion before them—trying to extinguish the sobbing that still mourned in recollection. She might not have been capable of recognizing Bus Crow in one split second even had he stood before her wearing the gray flannel suit she remembered so well.

He lifted his newspaper higher, but constantly his eyes watched above the margin of the sheets.

Still Mattie wrung her gloves, she had them both off now. With face distraught she turned from the lobby and gazed out of the open door at the end of the hall. Her expression was altered; but from where he sat, Buster Crow could not witness the transformation.

On the sunlit wooden sidewalk near a horse-rail, a little boy had appeared; his dog was with him . . . *I had*

154

one friend, though—wonderful—the best friend in the world. His name was Brownie. . . . This dog was a mixed collie and shepherd, brown-and-white, panting, his jolly tongue hanging loose like a strip of pink ham.

Yes, the boy was fastening a remarkable harness of ropes and straps around the dog, though face-licking operations interfered. Now he had dragged up a home-made cart, built from a wooden box, and his dirty hands strayed seriously about their task of uniting harness and cart . . . *they're just movers, Brownie, they're going out West . . .* and where were the two boys following along with the shotgun? Perhaps a better God presided now; perhaps the boys would not come.

Speedy Rochelle descended the stairway. He had put on his coat when the clerk emphasized that it was a lady and not a man who wished to see him. All of the self-appointed female informants who had come to him before this were ugly harridans—professional snoopers, women whose thwarted energies glued them to treacherous windows as they peeked out at the world and dreamed of the worst and happily anticipated it.

Rochelle was unprepared for a visitor of Mattie MacLaird's type. He could not believe that she might offer any evidence of importance; yet when he saw the intense misery in her eyes, he thought suddenly that perhaps—

"Did you wish to see me, ma'am? I'm Marshall Rochelle."

"I—I thought that maybe I—" Her gaze fell away, it wandered as her voice wandered. There was some rejection and alteration . . . Rochelle was perforce a student of physiognomy, and Mattie MacLaird had no poker face.

What did she see outside? A boy and a dog, the boy with his arms around the beast. . . . It was a good thing to witness—this communion of higher and lower orders —but it told nothing to Speedy Rochelle.

"Can I be of service to you, ma'am?"

Her whisper said sharply, "No! I thought maybe— maybe I had some information for you. But—" The artificiality of her laugh was apparent. "It was silly of me. I realized suddenly there was nothing I could say to you. Nothing important."

The marshal caressed the bullet on his chain. "Perhaps you might let me be the judge of whether it was important, ma'am."

"It was nothing. Do you understand? Nothing!" and her voice broke apart.

She hurried through the doorway away from Rochelle, hastening into sunlight, and briefly she stopped for a moment and stood looking down at the boy and the dog. The child arose as if in response to an unglimpsed signal. He had tried to fasten the cart, but could not make it work; perhaps repairs were necessary. He ran away down the sidewalk, dragging the crazy vehicle with bump and clatter behind him. The dog scampered after, its loose harness flopping.

She had something to tell him: Speedy Rochelle knew that well enough. She had not told. He turned back toward the staircase with a leisure that belied his perplexity. He climbed into upper shadows, twirling the bullet as he went.

In the lobby, Bus Crow got up and went forward. He folded the newspaper and tossed it upon the long table. Standing well within the door, he could see Mattie MacLaird as she untied her horse from the rail and mounted. She rode hastily up the street without a backward glance.

If Crow had been able to overhear her brief conversation with the marshal still he would not have understood the motivation of her attitude. But he had seen enough: he had seen her come into the hotel, send for the marshal, exchange a few words with him, and then vanish. Thus she was armed with a menace he had not believed that she might own . . . *sixty-seven men* . . . *killed seventy-one* . . . *you heard me.*

Bus Crow now hated himself for his sufferance, his melting. Deeply he cursed the advice given him in the letter—that advice which had sent him stalking toward the Elk Run School less than a month before.

His own horse was tied at another rail before a restaurant in shade across the street. Bus got his horse and followed Mattie. She was only a muddled speck at the end of the street by the time his feet were in the stirrups . . . he followed her out of town.

Within a mile the woman looked back and saw him coming, and speeded up her horse. There were other people on the road; Crow dared not appear too obviously in pursuit, yet he pressed ahead. He lost sight of Mattie in the narrow chasm along Milk Creek; she even left the road and turned up a lonely gully, hoping to vanish, but a child could have followed her; hoof marks were deep-pressed in the clay. Crow was galloping hard during the final minutes of the chase, but soon he caught her amid the rocks.

Twenty-Three

Freshets had torn the ravine to pieces, and Mattie's mare was a staid creature, good enough for road-work and for jogging over flat prairies, but inexperienced in the antelope activities of the range horse. The mare slid and stumbled for some distance before eventually she fell, but fall she did. She rose, smeared with greasy clay, and ran a little way; she stopped and looked back whimpering.

Crow did not see the tumble but he heard it. He streaked around an embankment in time to see the horse still galloping, and Mattie for the moment motionless, nearly stunned. Some decency ruled Bus Crow just then; he was on the ground in an instant, and had drawn the woman to her feet, but not as if he wished to strangle her.

Her clothing had been torn by the fall, and the flesh of one elbow was scraped raw: it showed through the rip in her sleeve.

The impulse toward tenderness (and it was only an impulse, fleeting as the fugitive swallows that swung startled from a cliff nearby)—this dissolved almost immediately, and Bus Crow's face was as implacable as it had been when he stood with Mattie in gloom beside the horse-trough.

He held her until he was sure that she could stand on her own feet. Slowly the clamp of his hands went loose.

"Are you hurt?"

"Let go of me. Oh God, let go of me!"

"You shouldn't have run," Crow said. "I want to talk to you. You ought to have known I could catch up. You saw the marshal. What did you say to him?"

She stared with raw gaze, she was staring past him.

"Come on, what did you say?"

"Something happened—I couldn't say a word."

"Why didn't you talk?"

She uttered another of those racking sobs . . . ordinarily he might have thought it was a horrid sound she gave, if not a pitiable one, but now he was impervious. She could not reach inside him (whatever claws she had possessed before) and steal an ounce of kindness from his spirit.

Crow asked roughly, "What did you see?"

"A little boy and a dog."

He pushed Mattie away from him. She stumbled amid a scatter of loose stones and they hurt her ankles as she stamped among them, though her cry rose from no pain as simple as that.

"I've got no strength," she gasped, "no decency! I'm a miserable— Oh, I should have told that marshal everything I knew!"

Bus Crow said that she knew nothing.

160

"Everything I imagined, I should have told him. Think of it: I let you touch me, I let you— Your filthy hands—"

His horse was standing close. Crow moved over to the horse and began adjusting the lacing on his stirrup strap: it was down a notch too long on the off side, and he wondered how that had happened. "Nothing you could say," he told Mattie over his shoulder, "would have made any difference, anyway. There isn't any evidence against me."

The woman's eyes were hysterically wide, yet no tears sprang from them, they were dry as crusts. "Evidence?" she repeated. "Who are you to talk about evidence? Women and children crying—isn't that evidence enough? An old man like Gus Bainbridge driving home dead in his buggy . . . and Davis Arden: you rode out there before sunrise this morning. You shot him in the back . . . another one of those foreign shells: it was lying beside him. Always those empty cartridges!"

He taunted her, "Where's the gun? Who's ever seen me with a rifle like that?"

"How do I know where the gun is? You've got it hidden somewhere. You were destitute when you came to town; you needed money . . . someone paid me to talk to you. Why? Just tell me that? Why did they leave that note, and have me tell you to go to the hotel?"

Bus Crow had been waiting for that question, and not only waiting on this day. "That's simple enough," he lied. "I did go to the hotel. Those folks had watched me playing blackjack; they saw that I knew cards pretty well. They wanted me to run a game for them, that's all. Well, I'm not a cheap gambler. Never was."

She cried (ignoring his falsehood, never believing him for a moment), "Now you've got money—plenty of money. Where did you get it? Who hired you? You're here, you're there, you're away from town for days at a time, you're vanished out on the range. Oh, yes, I know—you ride into town, your horse has been ridden hard . . . and then somebody's found lying dead somewhere. Oh, God, if I'd only been brave enough to tell the marshal about your sixty-seven men and your seventy-one men! Were they all men?" she sobbed. "Did you ever kill a child?"

At last she was assailing him with an agony abrasive enough to barb her words and make them sting. His face colored. He snarled, "I shouldn't have got soft with you."

"*You* shouldn't have got soft! I pitied you— I— loved you. Why did I do it? I'll always be dirty—"

Sunlight . . . the watching horses poked disconsolately among rocks, hunting for a few curled blades of grass. An acid of rage burnt in Bus Crow's nostrils. He advanced on the woman, he spread his hands and clapped them tight against her head.

"What's to stop me—" he ripped the words from his throat— "from twisting your head off your shoulders right now?"

"Nothing," she whispered.

She stumbled when he shoved her again . . . she knew that she stood very close to death. Mattie had never seen such concentration of hatred in any human eyes.

162

She remembered that weasel, a month earlier: it had been killing Mrs. Mason's chickens, and the old man set a trap. She remembered the weasel in lantern glare before Mr. Mason dispatched it with the blade of a shovel . . . Mattie had covered her eyes . . . teeth that bit the trap, the horrid feral screams and champing.

Bus Crow ripped open the flap of a leather saddle-pouch fastened beneath and behind his saddle. He drew out a flat whiskey bottle, pint size, as yet unopened; he held the bottle as if he would in fact break its neck. He would snap and sunder from it the life it had never owned.

His hands solidified around the bottle; the knuckles paled, then came a snap and shattering. The hands separated, the fingers of Crow's right hand retained the shattered neck and cork. There began a slow trickling of blood from his fingers. Dully Mattie saw before her a monster whose true proportions she could estimate for the first time.

Bus Crow tossed the neck and cork away, he lifted the broken-necked bottle and began guzzling whiskey, gulping swallow after swallow. He lowered the bottle . . . his mouth was bleeding too: slivers had pierced his lips even as he sucked the liquor down. Crow blinked tears from his eyes and swabbed his face with his right hand; thereupon fresh blood was smeared across the upper portion of his face, it was spreading like ink. He said nothing; he breathed heavily, gazing at Mattie.

And this was the face she had held close to her bosom. Behind that mask there dwelt the spirit which for a few hours had caused her soul to sing. *It isn't he,*

163

she thought, *he's—he's different, he's inside somewhere, hiding behind all that horror.* Perhaps she could reach out to him.

"Bus," she whispered.

The man drank the rest of the whiskey from the broken pint-flask. He emptied the bottle and flung it over his horse . . . a million miles away it went to bits among the rocks.

Once more he wiped his face. He was marked with worse pigment than was worn by countenances of the Blackfeet (now remembered only by boulders in dry watercourses where their bones were hidden).

Crow said, as distinctly as ever Mattie had heard him speak, "I never want to see you again," and there was darkness before her eyes. But through it she saw him grasping the horn of his saddle and swinging astride once more.

"Hear that?" he asked. "Never want to see you again! You or anybody like you."

Words poured with increasing heat and rapidity, along with the red spray that flew from his lips. "I never want to see *them* . . . I don't want to hear that voice in the bucket. Evidence? The hell with evidence! I'll throw it in the river; they'll never find it." Again the dark crimson swabbed wide as he wiped his mouth with the back of his hand.

"Want me to kiss you goodbye again?" He had turned his horse, he was riding—not back through the gully where he had come, but climbing the opposite side of the little canyon.

164

Mattie gazed until Buster Crow had gone over the crest. She could not move, she could not pull her eyes away, she could only stand and stare. She did not faint until he was gone.

Twenty-Four

Gare Stiver sat on horseback beside the narrow corral, its posts new-planted, its poles showing in places the bark still green. Behind him his son Willie was closing the gate.

"It's a big help," said Gare, "school being closed to-day. Now listen careful, boy. You'll have to go afoot—"

Willie glowered.

"That's all right, too," his father told him. "If we was rich folks, we'd have plenty of horses to ride. But we're not rich. I'll take the low ground—I can cover it faster—and you work the hills."

He sighed as he turned his horse away. "Look careful. I don't know just where that cow could have dropped her calf; but we can't spare even one calf to the wolves."

For the next hour and a half Willie combed through underbrush and over flinty ledges of the hills adjacent to his father's place. Despite his sullenness at having to trudge on shank's-mare, he found at first a certain excitement in the search. The mention of wolves helped. Willie imagined himself finding the weak little calf, damp and forlorn in a canyon, beset by the formidable approach of be-fanged gray monsters.

He built a thrilling picture of himself wrestling the wolves away from the precious toddler, fighting them off with fists and strangling and cleverly-hurled stones until they fled limping, their tails between their legs. The fact that Willie would have raced for home if the howl of even a small-sized coyote issued from the wilderness in his vicinity did not complicate his heroic musing.

The boy's journey took him across a succession of dismal plateaus, along crests of minor precipices. He tired of the calf search before long; he could not have found the animal without fairly stumbling upon it. He trailed on in desultory fashion, dreaming of candy and soda water (he would achieve these dainties if allowed to accompany his father to Pearl City on the following Saturday, and if he could wheedle a dime from him).

Willie entertained consideration also of the narrow-eyed, pig-tailed girl who sat on the other end of his bench at school—who had flushed in mock resentment the day before, when she caught Willie displaying interest in the round little calves of her cotton-stockinged limbs.

These temptations of the flesh distracted him. Then he thought of looking for gold. Rumors still flitted over the plain; there was talk for a boy's ears to catch . . . Willie was always ready to listen, if he could do so slyly as a gratification of his native sneakishness. People said that honestly there was gold—perhaps a whole mine of it—somewhere in Pearl County. Buster Crow, the dangerous man who had slapped Willie, was said to be searching for that very mine.

167

These reflections were muddled with other discussions Willie had heard about the peculiar foreign cartridges found in each case beside bodies of murdered men. Thus occupied with notions of treasure and homicide, Willie Stiver progressed toward the lonely extinction awaiting him. His very moments of breath were now numbered; but like every marcher in the pageant of mankind, he felt himself eternal—bound in godly armor, unconquerable by the forces of dissolution.

And here were more rocks: an interesting outcrop of spangled quartz. This very mica over which the boy now traced his grubby hand might be gold of a sort. Willie leaned close, examining glittering spangles in the stone. Some movement on the slope that fell away beyond— some shaking of bushes, the sharp click of stone on stone—caused him to lift his eyes. . . .

There were the thoughts he had had. They did not stay with him to the inevitable termination, but he had trouble brushing them away now . . . gold . . . if that ledge contained gold, he would pry it out; he would bring tools stolen from his father's little shed. He might even steal dynamite somewhere and set it off— that would be joy. He envisioned himself with a heavy salt-sack in hand. He would dump out his sparkling hoard when he brought it to the bank in Pearl City . . . men would gasp to see him with such wealth. "Boy alive," they'd say, "where did you find it?" He would smile at them shrewdly. "Mister, that'd be telling."

They would give him gold for gold: heavy minted coins, column on column . . . he would saunter to Partman's candy store, and then perhaps to the watchmaker's shop where there was a case of genuine jewelry. He might buy a present for the girl at school. Edda May Pursell was her name; and surely Edda May would appreciate a locket, a string of pearls perhaps, or a diamond ring. Since he had gratified her in this way, she might gratify him in turn, and not pull down her calico skirts so hastily. . . .

The slope beyond. What—?

The horse he recognized first: Buster Crow's chestnut. Willie knew—he had used brush and curry-comb on that very animal, he had lugged water—

The horse stood with trailing reins, knee-deep in scrub; near at hand knelt the master. Crow was on his knees in a slight depression of the hillside, sheltered by bushes. He lifted up good-sized rocks—rolling them aside, pulling out bunches of dry sage and tossing them out of the way. Other than this Willie could not see exactly what Buster Crow was doing.

He fell into a crouch and stole forward, playing already with the conception of himself as an Indian. On hands and knees he crept to his doom, lying low behind the sage at one time when it seemed that Crow was about to rise and face in his direction.

The boy crawled until he had reached a sharper lip of the slope. There were only sliding gravel and loose stones at this place, and no more growth—no more weeds and twigs for concealment. Willie could go no farther, but he could elevate cautiously on his haunches and see what was happening below.

Wall-eyed above the bushes, he gazed in disbelief. The treasure . . . could this be treasure? Bus Crow had dragged a big tin box from a hiding-place under stones and brush. It was of the sort in which workmen kept their tools when they dug the water-main in Pearl City streets: long, narrow, flat. There was a flange and padlock, and Crow had unfastened the lock. He threw back the lid.

Blankets appeared, and a frying pan, a coffee pot, a few tins of food. From among these articles Crow dragged out a narrow parcel; it was wrapped in his slicker. He unwound the bundled oilcloth, and there was white cloth underneath. He ripped it off; blue steel and polished woodwork shone.

Then and there the believable discovery shaped itself in Willie's brain. It was as if he heard words spoken aloud inside his skull, though he did not actually utter them. "Bet that's the foreign rifle. What you bet? . . . The gun. . . ."

He supported his body on stiff-elbowed arms, on hands with fingers spread. He craned forward, trying to catch a better view of the weapon in Bus Crow's hand; and thus his weight was too much for a stone where his palm pressed hard. A rock about the size of a man's fist tilted loose from the mass and bounded noisily down the hillside.

It was when Bus Crow jerked his head in the direction of the sound that Willie's fate was really sealed. Crow's face was still painted with blood, though the blood had dried. Not in any distorted imaginings of Willie's had Sioux war-paint looked as ferocious as this.

Then the boy was on his feet, jouncing up the slope,

and making not even a squawk of infantile alarm as he died. Something took away his breath—that was all he knew. A board struck him across the back with a rending blow fit to break his body in two. It felt something like the time in the livery barn when the brace which held the shafts of a surrey had slipped out, and Willie had been struck and injured. Surrey, the surrey . . . he smelled oats again . . . he wished desperately that he was at home to be comforted, because this wilderness— The blow made him gulp for air; he could not find any air. He thought that he screamed, "Mamma!" before blackness possessed him, and in fact he did give vent to an *M* sound, low and pitiful, the only sound he made. He left no whoop of death to trail its echoes across the hill where the *spank* of the Mannlicher was still bouncing.

Buster Crow toiled up the hillside, rifle in hand. He had fired automatically. A prowler was close, observing his secret, so he spoke the only remonstrance natural to him. The figure had seemed very small and very skinny but it wore a man's hat . . . the vague notion of Willie Stiver planted itself in Crow's mind before he reached the scene and stood looking down at the tumbled body in its dirty shirt and dirtier pants, spread among sage in the flattest disarray imaginable.

Quite automatically Bus Crow's hand turned up the bolt of the gun and drew it back; the shell flew loose. He was possessed, in the next instant, of a repugnance never felt before. The whiskey, he thought . . . Jas. Cannon's Sour Mash . . . should have put back that bottle I took out of the box . . . his stomach roiled within him.

He thought dully, "I was going to get rid of the gun anyway. Oh, the hell with it!" He lifted the rifle in both hands and smashed it down among jagged rocks beside Willie Stiver's body. There was still the sun of afternoon around him; if it had been dark, sparks would have flown fiery when that good steel drove among the stones.

Crow turned away blindly. Within two minutes he was in the saddle and riding hard. Water still stood in the deeper holes of Milk Creek . . . he halted once to wash his face and hands. He used up his handkerchief and threw it away. He took off his necktie and used that, and then rode on.

. . . Hours afterward the wolves talked around Willie's lonely body, and birds were out in full force as the sun grew hotter the next morning.

Speedy Rochelle and Sheriff Ballantine and another man joined in the search for Willie, halted their horses in silent and mutual command; they looked up at the sky ahead. They had come to the end of their search. They rode on, to climb past declivities and join Gare Stiver and a couple of friends in that horrid place where Stiver himself had arrived only a few minutes earlier.

Hastily the neighbors spread their saddle-cloths over what was left on the ground; the father crouched near-by, whining. He could not speak as tears found their way through sweat and stubble on his cheeks, but he did

172

utter a constant and inarticulate sound which the others would hear for a long time.

A man offered the Mannlicher to Rochelle. As he held the rusty weapon in his hands he recognized that he had been correct in his original theory about the box-magazine marks on those cartridges. The shield or bracket sustaining the magazine was itself bent awry, there was a crack in the stock, the barrel was half-turned out of the clamps which held it.

Old Ballantine wheezed behind the marshal: "Meant to tell you before we left town this morning—kind of forgot in this excitement— Fellow told me he saw Bus Crow get aboard the Denver train at Sears Junction late last night."

"Good town—Denver," said Speedy Rochelle. "I haven't been there in quite a spell myself. You like oysters, Sheriff?"

Ballantine stuttered, unable to comprehend the words he heard.

"At the Emperor Hotel in Denver," Rochelle told him, "you can get some mighty appetizing oysters. Expensive, but nice. They ship them in from the East—keep putting ice on them all the way, I guess. I haven't had any for a long time."

Twenty-Five

Sure (said the boss-waiter in Paddy O'Connor's Corner, The Biggest Little Place in Denver, to Speedy Rochelle and the men who accompanied him; and he said it on the third evening following the discovery of Willie Stiver's body)—sure, I think I know the geezer you mean. He was in here about two hours ago. Big and kind of dark; looked like a dago or something, only a lot bigger. Yes, he had black hair. No, I don't know what color his suit was—sort of dark. It looked like a new suit, but it looked like he had been sleeping in it. Maybe we oughtn't to have let him in at all; but he seemed quiet when he came. Yes, that's right, that's what he asked for: Cannon's Sour Mash. He sat right over there; that's the table, we got it cleaned up now. He seemed kind of dazed or something. He had maybe a couple more drinks before he went out. He didn't talk to anyone else. Sure, he was all alone: just sat there at that table and drank whiskey. Then Clyde here, he was waiting on him, and— What did he give you, a twenty-dollar bill? He gave him a twenty-dollar bill, and Clyde went to get change. You know, mister, like it is now— quite a crowd in here—kind of a family place, with folks laughing and talking, and some of them still eating their suppers a couple of hours ago. That was the damnedest thing: he was just sitting there, not looking at anybody much—just kind of staring ahead of him—and then Clyde here came up with the change and put it down in front of him. Do you want to know what that geezer did? Well, he picked up all the bills and put them in his pocket, and he left the silver laying there on the table. I guess Clyde had fetched a couple dollars in silver, and then all of a sudden this man, he just stands up and he upsets the table—bottles, glasses, salt, the tablecloth—everything goes. Just gets up, and when he gets up it's like the table gets up with him: everything falls down and smashes, and he just keeps walking. Walked right out the door there. Some of the boys started after him, but there were still a lot of folks out in the street that early this evening, so I called the boys back. We don't want no trouble on the sidewalk in front of the place. Paddy wouldn't like that, and he's home sick with the pleurisy. We run a quiet place, mister—you can see for yourself. But that was the damnedest thing. . . .

. . . You bet your boots (said the bartender at the Denver Drovers' Paradise), I certainly do! What are you, an officer or something? Well, anyway, you should have been in here an hour ago. Yes, it must have been the same fellow you're looking for: great big man—regular pugilist, looked like. I think he was wearing a gun—I'm not sure. Well, by God, he came in here and came right up to the bar; stood just about where you're standing now. No, I can't say for certain he was wearing a necktie. No, now I think of it, I know he wasn't: just his collar—you know—with the collar-button sticking out here on the front. He had a fairly good suit on, kind of messed-up, and he wasn't too well shaved. But lots of these customers—you know how it is—I haven't worked at a place like this all my life; why, I used to tend bar at the Palmer House in Chicago. Yes, I did. Two-and-a-half years, that was. Well anyway, this other fellow was standing right over there when your man came in. He was Mr. Matherly, owns that brickyard up the street. No, I guess he doesn't own it, but he's kind of a manager or something. Well, this Mr. Matherly—he's a very quiet gentleman, very well-behaved: one of the nicest-behaving gentlemen that comes in here. You know this isn't what you'd call a swell place, but we like to keep it decent. Well anyway, Mr. Matherly was standing right there drinking a gin fizz, and we were talking a little about politics. Yes, we were talking about Billy Bryan, and all of a sudden this fellow turned around and said to Mr. Matherly, "What did you say?" Well, Mr. Matherly was kind of taken aback, naturally, and he just said, "Why, I didn't say anything. That is, to you. I was addressing my friend the bartender here." Then your man said, "Don't you get gay with me," and Mr. Matherly said, "I'm not getting gay with you." Why, Mr. Matherly, he's only a medium-sized man—quite small—not much more than half the size of your man. And he hadn't any more than said that when this other man—your man, I mean—hauled off and gave him an awful swat. Knocked Mr. Matherly down, right alongside the bar

176

—right here in front of me—and I think he hurt his shoulder pretty bad on the rail too. Well, believe me that was all we needed. Those boys out there—that's Pedro over there with that tray full of ale now—and Tiffy—that's that big red-faced fellow wiping off the table back yonder. I don't know—I guess Ed and Leo were in on it too. Well anyway, they just moved in on your man right quick: three or four or five of them. They had him out of here so fast it would make your head swim. You bet your boots these boys in here know how to handle people like that. They all got right on him from the back, like a wrestler. Tiffy had him by the coat and collar, and they run him right out the door. I couldn't see past the door, but they told me they threw him clear across the sidewalk, big as he was. Of course he was pretty drunk to begin with. Maybe I shouldn't have served him; but we get a lot of drunks in here. I'm pretty certain that was the man you want. Just about an hour ago.

Twenty-Six

Her negligee was stained, her face scarred, she grinned lazily out at the world from a couch of battered purple grapes. What brushes ever put her upon that wall might not be known. A better-than-journeyman painter had traced his pigments on the plaster when the Forest Grove Saloon was another sort of place . . . old, lush days perhaps, before all the rich metal was sifted thickly out of the mountains nearest Denver—when people clinked their double-eagles on the bar where now they came with fifteen cents. Still the blonde trollop smiled her invitation, still she held the glass of rich red wine on high.

Buster Crow bulked against the bar, watching her. They owned no Jas. Cannon's Sour Mash in this dive, though Crow had demanded it. He had to be content with a cheaper and sharper brand, he had to be content with the entire smell and aspect of the Forest Grove Saloon. His condition was such that he could enter no better bar, though he had tried.

His collar was gone, and the round brass dot of the collar-button stared like a nasty eye in the soiled band of his shirt. Crow had come that way through a street where prostitutes wandered and a few panhandlers still crept; he had stepped across men sprawled over gratings and broken steps—not recognizing that likely enough he woud join them soon in their sidewalk slumbers.

Now he had found Her, and She seemed nagging even while She tempted. Perhaps She sought to berate him because his face was bruised and he had one sleeve torn out of his coat.

The sottish bartender stood half asleep, not energetic enough to wipe the bar or remove the scatter of glasses left by others. A few customers were in the place; they slouched together at a table or two . . . some slept solitary, or listened dreamily beneath the hiss of gas to the efforts of a pimply boy fifteen or sixteen years old, who tapped his fingers on the keys of an ill-used piano.

. . ."'Tis my own dear Jack," he whispered,
"I thought him safe at home."
"Forgive me, Father, but I ran away. . . ."

Coming up across the dim street outside, Speedy Rochelle and his two companions halted beyond the curb and examined the windows with their sagging curtains burnt to soiled peach-color by the lights inside. They read the sign.

Rochelle had donned a white collar in deference to city deportment. His face was serenely grave in the gloom, for a sixth sense suggested that this might well be the end of his night-time journeyings.

The other men with him were slender, taller than

Rochelle, and vaguely clerical or scholarly in their appearance.

"This could be it."

"Think so, Marshal?"

"If it isn't, it won't take long now. He's left an easy trail—broken glassware all over town—" He led the way to the front door. They entered unobtrusively, and immediately Rochelle could see Bus Crow holding himself against the bar, lost in secret communion with the battered mural opposite.

The bartender approached them, walking as if his feet hurt him terribly, and they did.

> . . ."Just break the news to mother
> And tell her that I love her,
> And tell her not to weep because
> Her boy's not coming home. . . ."

The other men sat down at a vacant table near the front, but Speedy Rochelle halted beside the bar; he glanced no more at the lone figure of Bus Crow far toward the rear.

"What you drinking, mister?" the bartender wheezed.

"Draught beer." He gestured aside—"For my friends, too," and when he had the stein in his hand, Rochelle began his slow approach of Buster Crow.

. . . Yes, she was Mattie MacLaird, though why she should be lying on that pile of grapes Bus Crow might never understand. She held her glass, she never drank from it, she was too busy talking to him. "You're sick,"

180

she whispered, and her face dissolved and wavered and then became warmly firm again. "It's just as if no one had ever been kind to you before," she said. . . .

The bartender-proprietor had served beer to the two men at the table and now he came back to his post among the bottles, wiping dirty hands on his dirtier apron.

. . . Mattie MacLaird's whisper was low and strong. "Did you ever kill a child?" she asked Bus Crow, and that was the last chiding she attempted. He shut her mouth for her quickly enough: the quart bottle half-full of whiskey was standing handy, and he fired it against her face before the words were scarcely out of her mouth. . . .

Behind him the piano tune stopped short. Patrons were startled, even from the depths of their dismal dreams. The bartender blundered angrily toward Crow, and never could he know why this stubble-faced brute sagged so fiercely against the bar, glowering at the great sunburst of brown wetness on the plaster.

The bartender tried to seize Crow by the arm. Without even looking at him, Bus swung his elbow in a single jab.

The man staggered back, hurt and frightened. His puffy eyes were pallid as the oysters Speedy Rochelle had talked about.

"I'm going to call the police!"

The marshal's deep voice was reassuring. "That won't be necessary, mister. I'll take care of him. He's an old friend of mine," and by this time Rochelle had his arm around Crow.

The killer stared. For a time he had difficulty in recognizing the marshal.

"Well you get him out of here! You can pay the damages, too."

Rochelle patted Crow's shoulder. Drawing away, he took out his wallet and extracted a banknote for the bartender. "Sure. An old comrade. We were in Cuba together."

"Well, take him back to Cuba!"

Bus Crow was trying to focus his recollection. "Cuba," he muttered, and then a vaguely-remembered slogan came to him and he spoke it. *"Cuba Libre. . . ."*

"Don't you remember me? Major Rochelle? We were at Daiquiri Beach. . . . Come on—I've got a nice little suite over here in the Emperor Hotel. We'll go up and have a drink."

By this time Rochelle's companions had slipped away through the front door. The bartender hovered opposite Bus Crow and the marshal, keeping pace with them as Rochelle welded Crow's arm within his own and drew the gunman down the length of the bar.

Speedy chuckled agreeably. "When old soldiers get together they ought to have a lot of drinks. We'll talk about San Juan Hill. Remember all those mules?"

Recollection was writhing to the surface of Bus Crow's brain. He could mutter, "I know you . . . Marshal. You can't take me in. No evidence."

Persistently the short man retained his grasp. The front door was not far away now; this would be less difficult in the darkness outside, and Rochelle thought he had seen a hack at the next corner.

182

"Evidence," he asked jocularly, "what evidence? We don't need any evidence to get you into the Emperor Hotel. Remember how you gave that idea to General Shafter about swimming the mules ashore? That was just about the cleverest trick in the whole war!"

With a culminating gesture of resistance, Crow jerked away, half-toppling against the bar, though he tried to draw his gun from the holster under his jacket as he tottered.

Speedy Rochelle chuckled again, and with ease he twisted the revolver from Crow's nearly-inert fingers.

"Oh, no," he cried, "not that. That's to shoot Spaniards with." He slid the gun inside his own belt.

"Remember that little *cantina* there at the crossroads? The people who got in there first—they drank up all the rum. Remember the straw around, and all the busted glass?" The only reply was Crow's own heavy breathing as he lurched obediently along with his fellow-veteran.

Twenty-Seven

Round and round the bullet wheeled. It was a strong chain on which the relic hung; Rochelle had broken the links twice merely because of the inveterate twirling his fingers made, and nowadays there was a swivel: the links would never break again.

Rochelle had put Bus Crow at an oval marble-topped table near the center of his parlor, and overhead a hanging gas-lamp sighed within the beaded fringe of its shade. Rays of light stung in smooth little circles around the brighter facets of the whirling chain; even the blunt granule of the leaden bullet lived within an aura of its own.

Bus Crow's hand was frozen around the tumbler of whiskey, and that glass was well-named: it had tipped more times than one. There were pools of liquor on the table, but Rochelle would say only what a shame it was . . . he had to bring another bottle.

Bus Crow's voice was weary and rusty. Still he struggled away from sleep.

". . . First time it was a Mexican kid . . . came at me with a knife."

"Oh, that was before you started killing Indians?"

"Killed a lot of Apaches—thirty-four that I know about."

"Bus, why did you kill Willie Stiver?"

Crow grunted heavily, still denying. He shook his head with stubbornness. "Never killed him."

"Just the same," said Rochelle cheerily, "we ought to have another drink. Old soldiers and everything—" He poured whiskey into two glasses.

"Don't you try to get me drunk." Crow downed his liquor and looked up with anger. "You drink, too."

"Of course! I always like to drink with an old comrade."

Crow's gaze drifted to the bullet spinning again from Rochelle's right hand. With his left hand, Rochelle tossed the whiskey out of his glass over his shoulder and heard it scatter on the carpet behind him.

"Who was it hired you, Bus?"

Across the room, behind Crow and to one side, the door of a closet was slightly ajar. One of Rochelle's two companions of the night was lying flat inside the closet. He lay on his stomach, with face near the aperture; his pencil whisked steadily across a stenographic pad. At the rear of the room a second door led to the bedchamber, and there waited the second court stenographer, listening and observing simultaneously.

Earlier in his career Rochelle had had some difficulty with evidence secured in this fashion; thus he was determined on a second witness to any incriminating admissions made by his victim of the night. As he stood beside the wet marble-topped table, and spun the bullet and droned his easy-going questions, he thought of

185

those busy lead pencils tracking across ruled paper. He found comfort in the justice of their attack.

"Hired me? . . . You mean—in Pearl City?"

"In the Continental House, wasn't it? I guess Crashaw came to see you."

"He took me to a room—I forget the number . . . but I couldn't see the man. He was behind a curtain."

"Well, you must have recognized his voice."

"He talked into a bucket . . . sounded funny."

Speedy placed a chair in comradely nearness to Bus Crow. "Remember how hot it was in Tampa before we sailed for Cuba? All those fat generals . . . we used to think General Shafter was going to melt away. The boys reckoned that he would be good, barbecued." He giggled at the thought.

He poured more drinks and sat down in the chair. "But it must have been pretty hot, too," said Rochelle sympathetically, "the day you got Carey Miller."

There were beads of perspiration on Bus Crow's face. His eyes drowsed, half-closed . . . bullet spinning again. "Yeh," said Crow. "Had to wait for him two hours."

"That black thing you wore over your face and over your clothes—you must have been really hot in that."

"Yeh. I didn't wear it any more after—after that next fellow—"

"You mean Bevin?"

With a supreme effort Bus Crow tried to lift himself from his chair and failed. "What are you trying to find out, anyway?" he mumbled testily.

Rochelle seemed fairly aggrieved. "Why, we're just having a friendly chat and a friendly drink! Let's have some more."

. . . They had some more—at least Bus Crow did—and the carpet was soggy behind Speedy Rochelle's chair . . . the second whiskey bottle lay upset on the floor, a third had been opened. The table-top was a mess of puddles, littered with splinters of glass. It had grown unseasonably hot, or so it seemed. Rochelle had his coat off by this time; he had put his gun away carefully, and the revolver which he took from Bus was also vanished.

In a lavatory at the farthest corner of the room sounded the steady trickle of water from a faucet. Crow had his arms folded on the table-top; he was falling asleep but Rochelle kept prodding him . . . the faucet was talking. . . .

"Can't you make that water stop?" came Bus Crow's weary prayer.

Rochelle apologized. "The plumbing's terrible here. Gets started running—you just can't stop it. But I'll try again."

He went to the corner of the room and made a pretense of working with the faucet. Still water came forth, curling across the lavatory bowl, gurgling where it first touched the discolored marble, and twisting with weaker noise into the hollow drain.

"Afraid that's the best I can do," said Speedy Rochelle, and he made bold to commune by gesture with the stenographers behind the half-opened doors before he returned, and they signalled their reassurance.

Something chilled Rochelle in the glance of these men. He needed them, he was depending on them; yet he was amazed (as he had been amazed before) to recognize that their prissy, correct honesty was a thin commodity when contrasted with the solemn, destructive avarice of the man at the table, pickled in the beverage of his choice.

With grimmest distaste Speedy Rochelle hated to admit the certain majesty which clung about a killer, whatever his degree of cold-hearted selfishness. He had roped Bus Crow at last; it was all in the bag; yet Rochelle knew he would never be able to point a finger of justice at the men who had engaged the assassin. Thus his satisfaction would be tempered by resentment against the fuller revelation he could not bring about.

Some disgust with himself was entering his voice, making it into a sharper, meaner thing.

"Let's get this straight now, Bus." He came back to the table and sat down. "You got six hundred dollars apiece for the others. How much did you get for Willie?"

Crow said sleepily, "That wasn't part of the deal— just an accident. . . . Guess it was the meanest thing I ever did." His voice drifted . . . surely he was sleeping.

By this time Rochelle had brought out a shining manacle; he was uncoiling a strong chain attached to it. "Yes," he agreed, "accidents are terrible." He leaned low alongside Bus and slid the open fetter around Crow's thick ankle.

"How do you feel, Bus?" he asked almost tenderly; but Crow merely grunted, and the definite click of the steel lock rang sharply through the high-ceiled room, tiny noise though it was.

"Come on, we've got to get going," said Speedy Rochelle.

Slowly the marshal's words seeped through Crow's blurry existence. He lifted his head, opened his eyes, tried to adjust his gaze; but his drinking companion, the table-lamp and all were a fog . . . they twisted in nightmare. Hammers pounded Bus Crow's temples with each pulsation of his veins.

"Yes, sir," said Rochelle, "we've got to get the early morning train for Pearl City."

Crow swallowed several times and gagged slightly. Rochelle thought the man was going to be sick then and there, and that would make it more difficult. Crow's hand found its meandering way to the good leather pouch on his belt: the revolver holster was empty.

He had a last combative impulse. With eyes protruding and face distorted, he tried to push back his chair and stand upon his feet—he even tried to make a fist—

Rochelle gave a sudden jerk, bringing his weight against the chain he had wrapped around his hands. Crow's ankle was torn from under him, and he fell heavily to the floor and smashed the upset chair as he went down.

The circlet of bright nickel clamped on his ankle. The chain extended taut to Rochelle's hands like a

189

rigid staff. Crow groaned and then rolled over, trying to cushion his head with his arm.

Speedy Rochelle's voice roamed off through the silence. He was quoting Bus Crow when he spoke. " 'The meanest thing I ever did. . . .' " he said aloud, but that was the only accusation he would bring against himself.

Twenty-Eight

For some months during the winter that followed, Mattie MacLaird wore daily a long apron of black sateen; and a pair of small bright scissors dangled at her belt. She had become a saleswoman in a Kansas City dry-goods store after being called back to Missouri in November by the last illness of her father.

Within a month following the arrest of Buster Crow, snow was caked on hills of the Shaving Kettle Range. The ice of winter would soon lock the Elk Run settlers in their houses or at least fasten them to their barnyards. There could be no winter term at the schoolhouse though it was contemplated for a time; but the structure itself had proved to be porous before the onslaught of wind and sleet. Roads would be drifted with snow through much of the season, and none but the larger children might dare attend in the bitterest months.

Mattie remained only briefly in Pearl City after the close of school. The news about her father—however disconsolate—came as a key to open the figurative prison where she cowered. She had to fight against a sensation of relief which in a more selfish spirit might have been transmuted into comparative ecstasy. She was glad indeed to be gone from Pearl City. The trial of Bus Crow was set for the first week of January; that was the week her father died.

Back in the Mid-west, word reached Mattie that the headlines of Denver and Cheyenne newspapers were studded with detailed descriptions of the trial's progress. Briefer versions found their way into columns of the Kansas City press. Her old landlady in Pearl City did the cruel kindness of sending clippings in every letter she wrote. Mrs. Ermels had heard vaguely of the first encounter at the Glad Hand; also she held garbled notions about Bus Crow riding home with Mattie in the Elk Run neighborhood: local gossips took care of that.

Mrs. Ermels wished to remind Mattie again and again of the terrible fate she had so narrowly escaped. *Ach,* she had been talked to by a Murderer; she had even been escorted to her home by a Murderer—though impelled to accept this attention by a species of neighborhood disaster.

"It makes me cold all over already to think how close you did come to being Murdered yourself, my dear Mattie," the old woman wrote. "Here is more clippings. A terrible man he is. The good God was protecting you Mattie," and more of the same.

Even after burning the letters and clippings Mattie could not get them out of her mind. They wheeled and merged in recollection—they clamored through her dreams. *BUS CROW TRIAL OPENS. Surprise Evidence Hinted By State . . .* she heard it all: the rising

192

babble of voices in courtroom and street, the rapping of the gavel, the repetitive examinations and cross-examinations of witnesses . . . *STENOGRAPHIC EVIDENCE ROCKS COURTROOM. Oral Confession Of Crow Secured Verbatim, It Is Claimed* . . . she peopled the witness-stand with men she knew. She saw them: Alesworth, Britton, Montgomery and others questioned by lawyers; Mattie MacLaird saw their faces . . . lips were moving, they were shaking their heads, and distant gobbled whispers swelled into the ominous rumble of an approaching Doom.

At first she thought she dared not go back to Pearl County. A Kansas City dressmaker offered her a position which might prove lucrative; wearily Mattie turned her face away from the west each time the gloom and brass of a winter sunset made itself felt through coal-smoke over Kansas City hills.

Yet there were other letters—the Christmas messages from her students. She kept these in a candy box; she got them out and read them sometimes at night in the boarding-house where she lived.

It was in the same boarding-house that a visitor left a copy of the Denver newspaper to which Mattie's glance went straying idly one February evening; and then she was frozen, her head at an uncomfortable angle as she read repeatedly the black type visible, folded over the arm of a platform rocker. *BUSTER CROW WILL HANG! ! ! Date Of Execution Set By Judge Cheever As Prisoner Stands Up Stoically* . . . Mattie MacLaird was sick. The stair carpet billowed to smite her with its faded green flowers as she toiled aloft to be sick, to lie weak and staring on her bed, to be sick again.

In any event she wanted to remain in Kansas City until the final ugly extinction had taken place; but the little smudged envelopes kept finding her there, undermining her resolution as surely as the wash of spring-time rains. . . .

"Dear Teacher: How are you? I am fine. You bet we are looking forward to spring term and our dear Teacher back with us again. Rosie has puppies now in a box, but Ma said she had them first behind the stove. . . ."

"Dear Miss MacLaird, wish it was time for spring term now and wish I could see you. I hope you are in good health. Papa and Jed and some other boys swept out the school-house yesterday they said, and they are going put in new windows too. I have got a little callender and I mark every day till spring term."

. . . Buster Crow would be locked away from her by the solidity of metal and brick. She would not be compelled to go often to Pearl City; she would never need to pass the jail when she went. She should try to find a strength and a lost delight—some decent purpose, some answer to the questions that cried in her mind . . . first spring grass of the range; larks of the new season whistling there, and even before them, blue-birds skimming from fence-posts. . . .

194

Mattie had eaten less and less; her fellow-boarders feared for her health, and prescribed tonics. She was thinner than she had been in ten years.

She went back at last—but to live with others than the Masons. She did not wish to stand in that living room again . . . surely her gaze would go toward the old couch . . . the stereoscope and its box of views would be lying there in sight. No, she would stay elsewhere.

She stepped once more upon the timbers of a platform built above the mud; she heard the squeals of children, their bodies were flung against hers, their sturdy small arms were wrapping her. Mattie had expected to hear the talk; she deadened her ears. *Didn't you read it in the papers? Of course the lawyers appealed, but it didn't do much good. They're going to hang him first week in June sure as shooting.*

Twenty-Nine

Sun of late May was warm on the bricks outside. It drilled through a dirty window behind Sheriff Ballantine's desk; it reflected through shadows and sparkled on rifles in the locked gun-cabinet.

Ballantine was examining the notices concerning three properties to be disposed of at a sheriff's sale, and was just about to post them on the outside door, when a deputy came to whisper that Mattie MacLaird had come.

"All right, send her in."

He arose stiffly as the woman entered. It seemed odd now to see her, sober in her dark-blue suit, unrouged, almost austerely polite. It seemed odd to think that less than a year before she had cried forth her ditties at the Glad Hand; and he, Ab Ballantine, had felt her lips touching the top of his bald head; and he had then romped away to waste five dollars on a box of candy for this charmer. It seemed odd. . . .

"How are you, Mattie?"

"I'm fine, thank you, Sheriff. How are you?"

"Oh, fine. Of course—you know—pretty busy with all these details to see after—"

He stood jingling some keys in his puffy hand, then hurriedly slid the keys back into his pocket. "You got my note all right?"

"Yes," said Mattie. "Yesterday. Of course there was school; I had to wait until today. Sheriff, I don't know why he should ask to see me," and she turned away.

Ballantine felt very uncomfortable about it all. He said pompously, "Well, he did ask. A dying man's request—Mattie, I didn't feel I could ignore it. Just the same, you don't have to go up and see him unless you really want to."

. . . Not even the ticking of a clock; only distant sounds of pounding and sawing, and a mumble coming through the wall where a reinforced door was barred and locked. They were building . . . *oh, no,* she thought, *maybe it's just men putting up booths for the fair, out there on the street somewhere. I remember I saw them when I came along. They're going to have baby-doll booths and wheels-of-fortune and everything . . . maybe Gypsy fortune-tellers, too, and sausages and lemonade and—*

She was at the window; the awful silence of the stuffy office came from behind to clutch her.

". . . Celebration, Mattie. Guess it'll bring a big crowd to town."

"Yes."

" 'First Annual Frontier Days Celebration,' " and the sheriff chuckled as he quoted. "Of course," he added hastily, "it was too bad about this—this other thing being postponed. I mean—the date of the execu-

197

tion. Sort of too bad to have an execution right the same time as a Frontier Days Celebration!"

"Yes."

The old man slid his thick arm around her waist and patted her. "Mattie, you don't have to go up and see him unless—"

"I'll go," she said. "Let's go right now. Can we?"

"You're the doctor."

He unlocked that door in the rear wall; then they were through the door and Ballantine was ushering her up a narrow stairway, and it seemed like the hullabaloo of sawing and hammering was all around them.

Barred door after barred door: *those are cells,* Mattie thought, *so that's what they mean by cells,* and she had never seen any cells before. She had never been inside a jail. Most of the cubicles were empty; there was an Indian asleep on the floor in one. In another an elderly hobo, forlorn in dirty undershirt, lay on a cot reading a copy of *The Wide World Magazine.* She would remember that always . . . *Wide World.* . . .

This was the upstairs—the second tier—and a narrow gallery led along in front of the doors. These cells were built around a court two stories high. A sheet of canvas had been stretched vertically in front of the cell where Buster Crow was incarcerated, to hold the erection of the gallows from his sight. It could not hold away the sound.

A single guy-wire extended down across the top of the canvas at a sharp angle, and was fastened to a steel eye-screw immediately outside the door: a screw anchored in bricks and plaster . . . and that wire vibrated as men worked on the scaffold beyond, and the sunlight sought to make rarity out of it. The wire quivered, dazzled. Mattie closed her eyes momentarily.

The slicing of wood, the pounding of hammers went on consistently beyond the shield. But the sheriff was close; Mattie could hear his gargled, "Here he is."

Ballantine moved away from her and toward the stairs. He turned once, and said in a stage whisper, "Just knock on the door when you want to come out." Then he went away speedily.

Within the door Bus Crow waited. His hands gripped one of the horizontal bars, his face was pressed close between vertical bars above . . . *yes*, Mattie thought, *I could use that to explain to the children about horizontal and vertical . . . could use a window-sash: it would be easy. . . .*

He was thinner; he had a two- or three-days' growth of beard. She had known all along that he would look like that: swarthy face turned pale as fish-flesh, deep eyes mourning out of their heavy-browed nests, and praying and seeming to give a false pity as always.

"So you actually had the nerve to come."

She said, "I had the nerve."

He nodded sharply, staring past her. "Did you see what's behind you—behind that canvas? Sounds nice, doesn't it? All that carpentry-work?"

"You asked to see me, Bus."

He cackled. "So I'm seeing you. You talked to the marshal, didn't you? Before he trailed me to Denver."

199

"Yes."

"You told him everything you knew about me—everything you thought you knew—"

The woman heard herself recounting: "That was after you murdered Willie Stiver."

"Oh," he cried, "I was drunk—I was kind of crazy—I didn't know what I was doing! But just one thing: Rochelle kept water running, when he got the story out of me in Denver. You told him about that—that—" He stammered for a moment, falling away in terror from the remembered sound, and seeming to paw around for an adjective of suitable ferocity. Obscenity would have been better . . . she was a woman—even though she—

What he finally found was *wicked*.

"You told him about that wicked water, too."

Mattie whispered in echo, "Wicked water. Yes, I told."

He yowled, "The woman with pity in her heart! You said you loved me. That's the reason I asked for you to come and see me. I wanted to tell you good-bye. Here it is. *Good-bye!*" and he spat directly through the bars.

. . . Halfway down the stairs she was conscious of her own footsteps tapping remotely beneath her skirts. It seemed that her legs were very long, and how could she balance on such a height as this and still keep walking?

She saw the gallows. The structure was nearly complete: an elevated platform had been built, with the tree and beam above. Three men were there, sustain-

200

ing the taller structure. On the gallery of the tier opposite Bus Crow's cell, across the court from it, two other
workmen were trying to secure a guy-wire like the one
already in place.

She saw them; she witnessed their twisting and turning; she knew they were looking at her. Of course they
had heard the bellowing of Bus Crow. Strangely Mattie
did not resent them.

For the first time in these months of agony she
could dream of freedom from an oppressive load. Bus
Crow's final act of hatred directed against her had
snapped the last strap which buckled her to the memory
of the grotesque and momentary love she had made.

The tap-tap of her heels struck a concrete floor,
she was on stairs no longer. She cared nothing for
the curious nudging and staring of the gallows-builders
behind her . . . the door ahead: it led to the Sheriff's
office.

She tried the knob. It was locked, she would have to
knock. But once through that door she might entertain
the illusion of a peace to come.

Mattie's hand slid into her reticule and found a
crumpled lace handkerchief. She put the handkerchief
against her lips; before she could knock, she heard
a key grating in the heavy lock. The door was thrown
open by Ballantine.

He stood aside as Mattie went out. With him were
gathered a group of men intent on entering the inner
court of the jail. There may have been faces Mattie
MacLaird could recognize in another time; she did not

recognize them in that moment . . . ah, they whispered, perhaps they nudged even as the workmen had done. Now they were behind, too, as so much of evil was fallen away after her. Here was the hall outside the sheriff's office, and the merciful blaze of day loomed beyond that.

Thirty

Members of the Stockmen's Club and
other citizens who had just passed
through the barred door into the cen-
tral area of the jail—these people paid scant heed to
Mattie. At least they appeared to pay scant heed.
But there was one among them who looked keenly after
the young school-teacher.

He remembered with sharpness how he had de-
cided that she should be an acceptable emissary to
carry his initial summons to Buster Crow. In recent
months this man had been so occupied with asserting
his denials of complicity—on the witness-stand and
off—that his present curiosity was a thing apart from
him—an almost clinical inspection of the woman, im-
passive, without emotion or more than momentary
speculation.

The sheriff led them on. He had locked the door
again, and with the group of eleven following him, he
approached the nearly-completed scaffold.

"This way, gentlemen. Want to show you how it
works."

They marched at his heels: the six who had plotted,
the mayor, a couple of county officers, a banker, a

railroad division superintendent in town for the day (who regretted volubly that he could not be there for the hanging when it took place).

"Maybe you remember," said Ballantine, "we had trouble in that last hanging—remember when we hung Blackie Anderson? Trouble with the trap coming open. Now I'll show you what I've got rigged up."

The men pressed together underneath the wooden platform, peering up at a roof of clean, yellow planks and the big metal tank bolted into place on a balanced cross-beam. Their eyes went over the mechanism: pipes, trigger, counter-weight. This was a strange device with which to project a spirit into oblivion. They were torn between admiration for Ab Ballantine's ingenuity, and inquiry as to where he might have gotten the idea in the first place.

"You see, we ran a pipe over here from the main water-system: it controls the flow that goes right into the tank."

Above them on second-story tiers the workmen still strained at their task. The screw-eye could not be secured properly on the east tier; they were wondering aloud whether the bars themselves—the frame of a cell now empty—could withstand the pressure.

A man worked his way over to the west balcony and examined the guy-wire outside Buster Crow's cell. His voice and the voices of others rang in hollowness above the explanation Ballantine was making to his visitors . . . *all right over here, Jimmy. Seems good and tight.*

Crow rested against the bars. Since Mattie Mac-Laird went away he had not altered his position except to lower his face. His eyes were closed, increasing his power of concentration, the receptiveness of his hearing.

Ballantine's elucidation sounded through clean-smelling boards and unpeopled space. One portion of Bus Crow stood ready to applaud the contraption the sheriff displayed: a pretty smart idea. . . . The rest of his spirit approached palpitating to his own inescapable fate. Already he shivered at the thought of water which would flow.

He knew the workman was there; he had heard him call.

Crow asked in a low tone, "Who's down there with the sheriff?"

"Bunch of folks just came in to see the—" The carpenter strangled, then managed to add, "To look at what we built."

"Who?"

"Bunch of those cattle fellows—you know, from the Stockmen's Club—you know. Alesworth, John Britton, Webb—that bunch," and his feet shuffled away. When Bus Crow did at last open his eyes the man had gone.

Far under the gallows-platform, Sheriff Ballantine exhibited a valve and explained how the immediate weight opened the trap and would force water into its first flow.

"When the weight of the tank over-balances that

iron weight over there, the trigger flops out and the trap falls free. Got it figured about right, I guess. He must still weigh close to two hundred."

The railroad man declared that this was ingenuity of the highest order.

"We'll try it tonight with sandbags," said the sheriff, relishing the prospect. "Ought to work all right. I sure do hate to have anything go wrong at a hanging."

Now they began to come out from the scaffold. Jaff Montgomery shook his head, and his sour voice spoke. It was pretty grim, he said, but justice was justice . . . a murmur of agreement found its way to Bus Crow's ears. They had all walked from under the gallows, and were moving toward the door.

John Britton spoke piously, "It will be a relief when this county is no longer soaked in blood."

Buster Crow clasped the bars as if to wrench them from their sockets. It seemed that he struggled for a long time to find his voice, to make it obey him, to twitch his lips apart and let his jaws operate, to speed vibrations in his throat that hummed into sound as the force of his lungs commanded.

"Yah," he hooted, "I heard that!"

The scrape of busy feet on the concrete was halted.

Crow had brayed above them so appallingly that they were rooted fast, and all gazing up. They could not see him, nor could he see them: the canvas was in the way.

The killer was fairly climbing the bars in a desire to send his accusation over and through the shield that hung between—to hurl a spiteful tirade into their faces.

206

His clawing hands twisted through the bars, his right hand was closed on the wire fastened beside his cell, though he did not know what he held.

He wanted to climb like an ape, to get nearer the top, to shorten the arc of his verbal fire so that it would strike the harder. With every punctuation of his speech he gave a lunge, throwing his weight against the stay.

"Who soaked this county in blood, anyway? It was you folks down there, and you know it. Six hundred apiece! That kind of money doesn't grow on trees. Who hired me, anyway? It was you rich sons-of-bitches with your fat bellies and your fat pocketbooks. You're as guilty as I am!"

All around the eye-screw, plaster crinkled; black lines of cracks zigzagged more widely; the cell-door clanged, the wire thrummed.

"Who was the man behind that curtain? Who talked into a bucket? Who hired me to kill the people on the range? Some bastard who didn't have guts enough to do his own killing! He got up on that witness-stand —he lied his head off—"

On the opposite tier three workmen held tightly to the guy-wire as yet unanchored. They stood transfixed in their observation of the prisoner's outburst. But now a foreman glanced quickly up at the towering structure of the gallows-tree.

With a grunt of alarm he plunged forward to lean upon the brace beside the other men.

Bus Crow's voice still shouted aloft.

"Who was it? I don't know . . . is there a God? Does

He know? He ought to wipe you suckers off the face of the earth!"

Still he climbed, and hauled his clutch upon the thin metal stay; still he howled and wished the whole world was there to hear him.

"Yes, yes, I did the killing, but you hired me! If I'm a murderer—whoever you are, you figured it out! You gave me the money. You're a worse murderer than I am. You can't forget it . . . you'll know it till the *day you die!*" and then the screw-eye shot out of the plaster like a cork from a bottle.

The visitors heard the warning creak, the grating of thick beams; their feet were glued to the floor . . . this could not happen. The structure of the scaffold was heavy and sound; they should know, they had just been under that platform.

Some men fell back upon others and they all went flailing toward the door. They tripped, their legs were intermingled, they were waving their arms; and the tall summit of cross-beams seemed poised motionless above, no matter how loud the workmen sang *Look out! Get back! There she goes, there she goes!* Then the timbers sank against them.

One scream that was more like a cat-cry stove aloft amid dust and splinters. It seemed impossible to believe that there could be so much dust in the jail (surely that floor was swept every day) and yet there must have been dust on the planks themselves.

Sun found rainbows amid the spraying motes. All the visitors were bruised and scratched, and one learned later that he had three toes broken, though at the time he thought only that his foot was sprained.

A lone man lay bent where the heaviest post cut its square edge across his neck and skull. They had to work for several minutes to extricate the dead body of John Britton.

Thirty-One

Amid music the wooden horses circled, and there were camels too, and one team of red-and-green chickens with gold-crowned heads. This was the gaudiest merry-go-round ever to be set up in vacant lots of Pearl City.

Mattie MacLaird progressed past the snake-charmer, the ice cream stands, the side-show where a barker snickered about the erotic charms within. She herded her children with her.

She wished only that the merry-go-round calliope would not keep calling its song . . . little horns coughing out the steamy notes amid a whirl of rocking animals. . . .

Two little girls in blue, boys,
Two little girls in blue.
They were sisters, we were brothers,
We learned to love the two.

Above their heads a wide canvas streamer sagged and flapped in the warm June wind: *First Annual Frontier Days Celebration. Rodeo. Calf-roping. Bulldogging. Fireworks.*

The crowd before the booths, the folks hurling base-balls and darts, the Indians munching cotton-candy out of cornucopias—there were not so many of these as would appear later in the day, for another attraction lured them afield. Nevertheless, some of the old pioneers were in evidence: men with long hair and silky goatees.

Mattie heard them talking, as two patriarchs hunted for change in front of the girly-girly side-show.

"Why, Jake, figured you'd be at the hanging."

"Naw. I've seen plenty of hangings in my time. This won't be no different."

She wanted to turn and cry that indeed this hanging was different—there would never be another like it—she wanted to cry, "When that trap goes down, I'll know that I can breathe again. There's a portion of my life that you don't know about. Nobody knows about it. It will perish when the trap falls, and then I can live again. I'll be a better human than I have been. Finally I've learned what to pity and what to despise."

This severe knowledge boiled up so heatedly in the woman's brain that she turned with an audible gasp to face the two old men in their weather-faded hats, though they did not even notice her. Smaller children clinging to her hands, holding happily beside her skirts, drew her on.

Ahead the merry-go-round circled to a halt, and several of the elder pupils broke away to sprint beyond Teacher and the smaller ones. They stampeded past the red ticket booth and were climbing astride gay-har-nessed steeds before Mattie had opened her reticule.

The shaggy old proprietor beamed at her. "Step up, folks. Step right up. Five cents a ride!"

She could hear little June Arden still marveling as Mattie counted off the long strip of tickets.

"Why did school close today, Teacher?"

"Because so many of the parents were coming to town, dear."

"Why were the parents coming to town?"

Mattie said (*by God,* she swore, *I'll say it if it stifles me in the saying*)—"Oh, I suppose it was because they wanted all you children to have a holiday."

June considered it still. "Did all the parents give you money to take us on the merry-go-round?"

"Yes, dear," and she felt the graceful springs within the little body as she gasped her dry laugh . . . her laugh ended in a bleating sound. She lifted June upon the red saddle of the chocolate-colored horse.

Truly enough the majority of the Elk Run parents were among the throng at the first corner beyond. They stood in vast assemblage, docile but staring, banked around sidewalks across the street from the two-story jail. Only a few people were gathered in front of a door that led directly to the sidewalk from the jail building. Deputies guarded there—men wearing guns and badges—and they had orders to keep the sidewalks clear. You had to have some remote claim to an official capacity if you were to stand close.

Inside the jail itself, witnesses shuffled in a hollow square around the gallows. Here were a dozen out-of-town reporters as well as the local witnesses selected; of course all were men. They whispered together; some were pale—and these were the ones who whispered loudest, to discount the trepidation that ruled them.

"Looks pretty strong," a reporter from Cheyenne gushed in Ole Paulson's ear. "Don't see how it could ever have fallen down."

"I guess this is stronger than the other."

"Wonder if that water-tank apparatus will work?"

"I bet you five dollars it does," said Ole, but the young reporter did not take the bet. He kept moistening his lips and wrinkling the pages of the neat little note-book in his bloodless hand.

In Buster Crow's cell, before the small procession turned out along the tier and headed toward the stair-way, the minister began to read excerpts from the Twenty-third Psalm.

This preacher was an earnest man, terrified and con-fused by the first experience of its kind which had come to him. He had been awake most of the previous night, trying to compose properly the Scriptural quotations, the prayers he would unloose.

At first his words were gibberish, but the clergyman gained courage: by the time the party descended into the open court and approached the gallows, every man waiting there could hear the intonation clearly. *Yea, though I walk through the valley of the shadow of death, I will fear no evil: for Thou art with me. Thy rod and Thy staff they comfort me . . . I will dwell in the house of the Lord forever. . . .*

A few people had not taken off their hats to begin with, but they removed them now. Some lips twitched in unison—men recited in a dragging whisper, echoing along with the minister the phrases they recognized, and thus they made an indistinct buzzing. But there was unearthly resonance in the preacher's later prayer. His voice went up hollow against the high ceiling of the brick room, and not even the scuffle of feet on the gallows steps could cope with his imploring.

Oh, Lord, we pray that Thou wilt take the soul of this unhappy man to Thy bosom: that Thou wilt show him the light which in his stubbornness he doth refuse to see. Oh, Lord, we pray that Thou wilt pity and comfort this soul as he comes to Thee, for Thy mercy's sake, in the goodness and mercy and eternal love of Thy sweet Son who taught us to pray: Our Father, which art in Heaven, hallowed be Thy—

Most of those present knew the Lord's Prayer; thus they pronounced it through all the shuffle, the whispered directions, the signals that passed among the few men standing on the platform. Now executioners had put the hood over Bus Crow's face, and things were easier: they did not have to look at his eyes. Matters were simpler for Crow as well; he waited in welcome darkness for the sound of water.

He heard it suddenly. The trap seemed to vibrate beneath his belted feet, and in the same instant it was a fact that Brownie was barking not far away. Crow heard an occasional cough or throat-clearing from the anonymous spectators; he heard the creak of their shoe-leather, too, and there was even the spatter of drops that flew against the edge of the concealed tank, that spilt in spray from a connection not turned tightly.

But over all these sounds (and the more important—the most important thing of all—the water gush) a murdered collie had healed himself of his wounds . . . he scrambled wet and shaggy through spring and ford alike, wheeling his burry tail like a bell-rope, clambering toward Bus Crow, demanding that Bus give up the intention expressed in reiterated conceit: *I'll kill, too. I'll always kill. I'll shoot them down . . . I'll shoot the whole world . . . get a gun and keep killing and killing.* The stream ran longer and thinner as the valve in the pipe began to close.

The dog was close at hand; Crow could smell his avid breath. He discovered he was dropping on his knees, going down to a lower place to put his arms around the animal. "Why," he thought, "I was right all along! Water can cure, the way I tried, the way I tried. Look, it *cured him,*" and then he was free in space, and silver light popped in his eyes.

. . . Some of the spectators were grimacing; some seemed faint; a man or two had turned away, though a few were actually leering. Behind them the door in the brick wall opened with a bang and was held ajar by deputies whose voices stung into the room, telling people to file out, one at a time. Calliope music of the distant merry-go-round came to greet them: *Two little girls in blue, boys—two little girls in blue. . . .*

Not much more than a block away, Mattie MacLaird came up to the retarded circle of gaudy beasts to extend her arms to lift children down from their last ride;

215

for all the tickets were gone, and some money must be saved for peanuts and cotton-candy.

June Arden wanted to know, "Aren't *you* going to ride on the merry-go-round today, Teacher?"

Mattie held her close. "No, darling," she said, "not today," and the calliope music piped louder than ever.

Now Available

MacKinlay Kantor
Pulitzer Prize-winning author of *Andersonville*

BASIS FOR THE FILM
THE MAN FROM DAKOTA

For more information
visit: www.speakingvolumes.us

Now Available

MacKinlay Kantor
Pulitzer Prize-winning author of *Andersonville*

Poignant, tender, and powerful, VALLEY FORGE brings into sharp new focus one of the most tensely dramatic episodes of the American Revolution.

For more information
visit: www.speakingvolumes.us